PUFFIN BOOKS

FRIGHT NIGHT

THE SHRIEKING STONES

'I don't care what you say; there's something strange going on,' said Adam.

'Well you'd know,' replied Lana, affectionately. 'Weirdo.'

Bowing their heads against the wind and rain, Lana and Adam hurried down the path towards Bray, not looking back. So when a bolt of lightning lit up the night sky, they didn't see the tall, dark figure standing in the centre of the Shrieking Stones, watching them

Books by Steve Rogers

Fright Night: The Shrieking Stones

Look out for the next
Fright Night book, coming soon

FRIGHT NIGHT

THE SHRIEKING STONES

STEVE ROGERS

PUFFIN

Published by the Penguin Group
Penguin Books Ltd, 80 Strand, London WC2R ORL, England
Penguin Group (USA) Inc., 375 Hudson Street, New York, New York 10014, USA
Penguin Group (Canada), 90 Eglinton Avenue East, Suite 700, Toronto, Ontario, Canada M4P 2Y3
(a division of Pearson Penguin Canada Inc.)
Penguin Ireland, 25 St Stephen's Green, Dublin 2, Ireland (a division of Penguin Books Ltd)
Penguin Group (Australia), 250 Camberwell Road, Camberwell, Victoria 3124, Australia
(a division of Pearson Australia Group Pty Ltd)
Penguin Books India Pvt Ltd, 11 Community Centre, Panchsheel Park, New Delhi – 110 017, India
Penguin Group (NZ), 67 Apollo Drive, Rosedale, North Shore 0632, New Zealand
(a division of Pearson New Zealand Ltd)
Penguin Books (South Africa) (Pty) Ltd, 24 Sturdee Avenue, Rosebank,
Johannesburg 2196, South Africa

Penguin Books Ltd, Registered Offices: 80 Strand, London WC2R ORL, England

puffinbooks.com

First published 2008
1

Text copyright © CPI Hothouse, 2008
All rights reserved

Set in Baskerville MT
Typeset by Palimpsest Book Production Limited, Grangemouth, Stirlingshire
Made and printed in England by Clays Ltd, St Ives plc

British Library Cataloguing in Publication Data
A CIP catalogue record for this book is available from the British Library

ISBN: 978-0-141-32372-5

With special thanks to Simon Forward

1

'*Action!*'

Larry Craddock turned to face the camera, one hand planted on his head in a desperate attempt to prevent his wig being blown off by the howling wind.

'Welcome to *Fright Night*,' he bellowed. 'This week we're in Ireland, at the Shrieking Stones of Bray. It's pitch-black, we're miles from civilization and we're absolutely alone – my instincts are screaming at me to run for my life. These ancient monuments stand at the meeting point of dozens of mystical ley lines. They're so filled with supernatural power that even if only half of what I've heard about them is true, my niece, nephew and I are in deadly danger.'

'Deadly danger of frostbite, maybe,' muttered the niece in question, Lana Craddock.

'Are you kidding?' replied her brother, Adam,

grinning broadly despite the freezing gale. 'This is so cool – our first all-night ghost watch!'

The pair were standing in the centre of a huge circle of standing stones. Admittedly, the towering megaliths provided a very dramatic backdrop, but they did nothing to shield them from the elements. Relentless rain fell from the starless sky, plastering the hair to their heads and trickling down under the collar of their anoraks. Adam's feet had sunk ankle-deep into a puddle of mud, while Lana was sneezing uncontrollably.

'In the Dark Ages,' continued their Uncle Larry, 'it was said that these stones formed a gateway into the very depths of hell. Standing here on a stormy night, that's easy to believe, isn't it, children?'

Adam nodded obediently as the camera panned over to him. Lana rolled her eyes – and sneezed again.

'And *cut*!'

Angela, the producer, looking considerably less damp than the rest of the crew in her designer wax jacket and sou'wester, bustled forward from behind a camera.

'Lana! Could you *try* to look a little less bored? Use your *imagination*, for goodness' sake.'

'It's freezing out here,' replied Lana, still shivering.

'Oh, *honestly*! Such a fuss over a little bit of rain. Where's your brolly, anyway? I hope you haven't lost it.'

The crew had provided Adam and Lana with an umbrella at the start of filming, but within seconds the wind had snatched it from them and sent it hurtling over the cliffs into the raging sea below. Now the pair wouldn't be much wetter if they had been dragged in for a plunge themselves. The difference between them was that Adam looked like he might be up for a swim, while Lana looked as if she'd rather be standing in a pit of snakes.

'*Right*,' continued Angela, as usual not waiting for an answer, 'let's move on to the next shot.' She consulted her waterproof clipboard. 'That's straight into your next block of commentary, Larry. So, Adam and Lana, you stay where you are, and Camera One, you go into close-up on the children, while Camera Two does a full pan around the stones.'

Camera Two – a man otherwise known as Dave – resembled a walking tent in his great plastic poncho. He signalled with a thumbs up.

'Right! *Action!*'

Uncle Larry drew a quick breath in preparation, then launched into his next speech.

'Gateway to hell or no, some people believe that standing stones such as these – scarred and pitted with the passage of centuries – act as powerful magnets to ghosts. Once a site for the living to gather in worship of their ancient gods, could they now be a place for spirits such as the Banshee of Irish myth to congregate and –'

Suddenly, from out of the stormy night, something swooped down upon Adam and Lana.

Out of the corner of his eye, Adam caught a glimpse of talons and wild yellow hair. He grabbed his sister and pulled her to one side, ducking behind one of the great stones for cover. Laying their hands against its rugged surface to steady themselves, Lana and her brother glanced frantically around.

As it arced round for another dive, they got their first proper look at their attacker.

Adam burst out laughing.

Flying through the air was what appeared to be a large rubber chicken with a beakful of matchstick fangs, a wig of yellow string and a pair of plastic bat wings Sellotaped to its back. As a finishing touch, the whole thing had been given a liberal coating of lurid green paint.

It was suspended by wires from a boom that

was still being swung this way and that over their heads.

'*Cut!*' shouted Angela, sounding about as far from amused as it was possible to be.

Uncle Larry wasn't seeing the funny side either. His face reddening, he pointed at the strange creature dangling limply above his head.

'*What*,' he bellowed at Angela, 'is that?!'

Always professional even in a crisis, Angela kept her cool. She clutched her clipboard against her chest like a shield. 'That,' she answered coolly and firmly, 'was a Banshee attacking you.'

Adam looked at Lana and they both shook their heads. They knew exactly how their uncle felt about 'special effects'. The fact that this one had been none too special could only make things worse.

'Angela, I thought I had made it abundantly clear – on numerous occasions – that I will not stoop to cheap gimmicks on my show! It's cheating the audience and I won't have it. It's real ghosts or nothing!'

'Yes, and it usually *is* nothing! We can't afford another dud like last week's episode. You can only go so far with atmospheric footage of empty "haunted" houses. Sooner or later you have to deliver something more scary than a creaky floorboard!'

'Poor Uncle Larry,' whispered Lana. 'Do you think we should say something?'

'Mum always said to stay out of other people's arguments,' observed Adam gloomily, leaning back against the stones. 'We'd best just –'

Adam felt a fierce cold course through his fingers. He snatched his hand away from the stone and glanced at his sister to see that she had done the same.

A hollow, reedy howl filled the air. It might have been laughter, but to Adam it seemed more like a threat. As the sound echoed around the stone circle, it seemed to linger near his shoulder. Or something did. Adam shuddered, as though to shake the presence off.

'What was that?' he asked.

'What was what?' replied Lana.

'Oh, come on. You felt it too. That cold –' he couldn't find the right word – 'shadow.'

'It's freezing, Adam. Of course I felt cold.'

'Yes, it's cold, but it was more than that. And anyway, I meant that voice.'

Lana cast her eyes around the circle of stones. 'Adam, we're in the middle of a film set. It was probably one of the crew laughing,' she said, with a tone that suggested she was stating the obvious. 'Carried on the wind.'

'No way. It was something else.'

'What, the ghostly voices of the Shrieking Stones?' Lana suggested, with a mocking smile. 'Yeah, right.'

Adam shook his head at his sister.

'*You* may not believe in ghosts, but *I* know what I heard. I'm going to ask Uncle Larry.'

But Uncle Larry was still rather preoccupied with his argument with Angela.

'And how did you ever hope to convince our audience with *this*?' he fumed.

'Well, a few decent reactions from the kids would have *helped*,' Angela returned, with a pointed look at Adam and Lana.

'How's this for a reaction?' Uncle Larry yelled – and he yanked the Banshee from its wire and tried to break it over his knee. Unfortunately, as it was made of rubber, temporarily bending it out of shape was the best he could do. Then it snapped back in his hands, slapping him in the face and sending his glasses flying. The fake creature lost several strands of its yellow hair and a selection of other features that had been stuck on.

Uncle Larry gave up and hurled it to the soggy ground in disgust.

For a moment, Angela stared, dumbstruck.

Then she let out a wail that even a real Banshee would have been proud of.

'That is *it*!' she cried. She rushed across the circle to pick up the rubber chicken, cradling it in her arms like a lurid green baby. 'You've ruined a very expensive prop. We can't *possibly* do anything else tonight.'

'It's just as well,' Uncle Larry replied grumpily. 'We are not doing anything else with that thing ever!'

Lana and Adam held their breath. In Angela's expression, there was the threat of a storm brewing that could easily outdo everything the weather had thrown at them. Uncle Larry and Angela stared at each other. For a moment, Adam thought that his uncle might finally stand up to the pushy producer. But under Angela's unwavering glare, he dropped his eyes.

'Well, what're you all loitering around for?' boomed Angela. 'Everyone, back to the guest house!'

Adam and Lana watched as Angela strode off, clinging to the Banshee. The rest of the crew were also trudging off, dragging lights and cameras after them. Soon, the children were alone.

'I think poor Uncle Larry's in trouble,' Adam remarked.

'And maybe us too,' Lana replied. 'Typical. I didn't even ask to come on this crazy ghost hunt.'

For the second time that night, a strange noise whistled through the stones. An eerie sort of chuckle that passed through Adam like a cold shiver. Again, it felt close. Much too close.

Adam searched around and then looked straight at his sister. 'Did you hear that?'

'Oh, Adam, cut it out! Let's go.'

Lana set off in pursuit of the crew, and Adam had to hurry to catch up with her. But he hadn't gone more than a few metres when the hood of his anorak suddenly flipped up, emptying half a pint of freezing water over his head.

'Argh! Did you see that?' he appealed to Lana. 'Something grabbed my hood!'

'Yes, Adam, it's called the wind,' she said, marching off again.

'*Hahahahahaha!*'

There was no doubt about it this time – the same sinister, hollow chuckle rose above the wind again. Even closer than before. Almost as though it was blowing in his ear. Adam looked around. Nothing.

'Come on!' called Lana from further down the hill.

Adam looked around again. Still nothing. Thunder rumbled above him, and the rain was getting harder. Whatever it was, Adam wasn't prepared to get even wetter finding out. He broke into a run to catch up with his sister.

'I don't care what you say; there's something strange going on.'

'Well you'd know,' replied Lana, affectionately. 'Weirdo.'

Bowing their heads against the wind and rain, Lana and Adam hurried down the path towards Bray, not looking back. So when a bolt of lightning lit up the night sky, they didn't see the tall, dark figure standing in the centre of the Shrieking Stones, watching them go.

2

At dinner, you could have cut the atmosphere with a knife. Which was more than Adam could say about his steak. He glanced enviously down the table. Mrs Flanaghan's Guest House hardly provided haute cuisine, but the rest of the crew all seemed to have something more appetizing on their plates.

Adam suffered his food in silence though, as Angela and Uncle Larry had brought their quarrel with them all the way back from the stones. Angela's withering glare, which she distributed freely round the table between mouthfuls of an extremely crunchy salad, was enough to make everyone wary of speaking.

For her, this was a working dinner: even before any food had been ordered, condiments and cutlery had been pushed aside to make room for her laptop, and she had the script spread open on the other side of her plate, a green felt-tip resting across the open pages. There was precious little in the way of elbow room, or much room of any other kind.

Adam nudged Lana and pointed to an adjacent table, where Steve was busy treating the rubber chicken to some makeshift repairs. As they watched, he came over to present his first efforts for Angela's inspection.

Adam couldn't resist. 'Would you prefer a leg or a wing, Angela?' he joked.

Angela shot him a glare that strongly suggested she was not a fan of his brand of comedy.

'Well, it's nothing like a real Banshee,' Adam complained. 'A real Banshee is a female fairy spirit. With dark hair – not bright yellow.'

'Listen to you. *Real* Banshees, indeed. You sound as batty as your uncle.'

Angela shook her head sharply at Steve and sent the man shuffling off like a schoolboy who had just been told to do his homework all over again.

'I don't know why you're fixing that thing up,' Uncle Larry mumbled. 'We're not using it in the show. That is, um, I'd really rather we didn't.'

Angela downed her fork with a bang. 'Larry, *darling*, I think it's high time you woke up to the hard realities.' She tapped her laptop screen. 'Listen to this – it's going to be in the paper tomorrow: "Two Ghost Shows Go Head To Foot In Ratings Battle",' she read aloud.

Uncle Larry's face fell. 'Who sent you that?' he fretted.

'Never you mind. I have my sources. "Head To Foot",' she repeated. 'That's the part you need to focus on. You see, it's a subtle play on words to show just how far below *Ghosts Unlimited* we're currently standing in the viewing ratings.'

Uncle Larry's face looked ready to fall some more, but as it was already in danger of hitting the table, he made an effort to sit up instead.

'Yes, I see that, Angela, but it's hardly a fair comparison. They have all that computer wizardry and whatchamacallit.'

'CGI, Uncle Larry,' said Lana quietly and, she hoped, helpfully.

'Yes, that. Thank you, Lana.'

'So you're planning to fight back with rubber chickens?' Adam blurted.

The look Angela gave him was by far the scariest thing Adam had ever seen on *Fright Night* – or any other show.

'Rubber chickens?' she repeated, flaring both nostrils like a dragon gearing up for an impressive spell of fire-breathing. 'That was an expensive *prop*. There are such things as rising costs. You get less Banshee for your pound these days.'

Uncle Larry nodded. 'Yes, I'm sure Adam didn't mean –'

Angela winced. 'Ow,' she complained. Then she scowled at Adam and Lana in turn. 'Whichever of you kids is swinging your legs under the table, stop it at once.'

'Adam!' hissed Lana.

'I never did anything!' insisted Adam, peering under the table. A cold tingle flashed down his neck and he froze.

Angela sniffed, unimpressed. She gathered up her script and started putting thick lines through several large chunks of text with her green felt-tip.

Uncle Larry cleared his throat, and for a while he looked like an actor who had forgotten his lines.

'Yes, well,' he said at last, raising a finger nervously, as though wary of getting it bitten off. 'Let's not forget that *Ghosts Unlimited* should be called *Funds Unlimited*. They have money. They can afford to be flashy and glossy. That's not our style. That is *not* what we do,' he insisted, making an effort to sound firm.

Angela paused in her ruthless work, clutching her pen like a small plastic dagger.

'No, we do *boring*. We do *dull*. And we do driving our viewers away in *droves*.'

'That's not fair!' piped up Adam.

The salt shaker and pepper pot toppled over with a clunk, spilling some of their contents in a white and sandy-brown pile on the tablecloth.

Angela shot Adam another deathly stare.

'Don't jog the table,' she told him sharply.

'I didn't!' Adam protested, throwing up his arms.

'Adam,' warned Lana in an undertone, 'stop it. You'll get us into more trouble.'

'*Hahahahaha!*' someone laughed.

But Adam didn't see anyone's mouth moving. He looked round, a nasty suspicion forming at the back of his mind.

'It's not funny, young man!' said Angela indignantly.

'Angela, please, there's no need to take things out on the children,' interrupted Uncle Larry.

Angela's nostrils flared again. She held up the pen as though she wished she could scribble Uncle Larry out of existence.

'Larry Craddock, I am your *producer*. Do try to remember who's in charge here.' The thinnest of smiles flickered across her face. 'It's worth bearing in mind that most of our budget goes on travel. The fewer people we have to cart around to all these "exotic" locations, the more we have to spend on other things.'

'You can't leave us behind!' objected Adam.

'Why ever not? A stack of DVDs and a takeaway menu should keep you happy and out of trouble. Larry's always saying how you can look after yourselves.'

'We can.' Lana nodded vigorously, seeing a chance to get out of future rain-drenched trips to the Shrieking Stones. 'We'd be fine on our own.'

Uncle Larry fidgeted awkwardly and cleared his throat.

'Now, Angela, you know I agreed to look after them while their mother and father are away. Besides, the children are part of our appeal. What better connection to our younger viewers than seeing two young, smart children confronting these *horrors* around the globe?'

'But *what* horrors, Larry, dear? We've not managed to turn up a single ghost or ghoul.' Angela put away the script, tucking her pen in her breast pocket. 'And if it weren't for you and these kids we wouldn't have to be trudging back up to the stones tomorrow night for a re-shoot.' Snapping her laptop closed, she reached for her fork and her bowl of salad. 'I don't care what expedition their parents have swanned off on. One more fiasco like tonight – one more disruption – and they are *both* on the first flight home.'

'No way!' cried Adam, banging his fist on the table. 'You can't do that!'

The small pile of spilt salt and pepper flew into the air. From nowhere, a sudden gust of cold air sent a spray of seasoning straight into Angela's face. She spluttered and gave in to a fit of sneezes.

Adam and Lana gasped, and they both clamped hands over their mouths in an effort to prevent themselves laughing. Uncle Larry's jaw dropped open too. His hand shot to his head to make sure his wig had withstood the gust. He patted it as though doing his best to calm a very flat pet.

Red-faced and furious, Angela leaped to her feet.

'That is the *last straw*. You two can go straight to your room. Right now. And I don't want to see you until tomorrow morning.'

'But –' Adam and his sister both tried to speak at once.

'Ah-ah!' Angela shut them off with an upraised

hand. 'Not another *word*! Consider yourselves confined to quarters!'

The twins turned to appeal to their uncle. But he just cast his eyes downward, looking very grave and refusing to meet their gaze. He reached for a glass of water. 'You'd best do as Angela says,' he croaked out, his throat sounding terribly dry.

Lana poked her brother.

'Now look what you've done!'

In truth, she was almost as angry with herself for having laughed. She should have bitten her lip and sat there looking suitably horrified. Now she had to cross the whole dining room with everyone else staring at her. It was *so* embarrassing.

If Adam felt embarrassed, he didn't show it. He was too busy scanning the room. He couldn't see anything, but as he reached the door he heard the unmistakable sound of someone – or some*thing* – chuckling darkly.

And as they stepped into the hall, a chill draught seemed to follow them out.

3

Lana was not happy.

She couldn't believe that she'd been sent to her room as if she was a five-year-old. All because of her stupid brother and his silly 'jokes'.

The room was small and simply furnished and there was something very old-fashioned about the flower-pattern wallpaper, but at least the window was double-glazed. So even with the rain lashing against the pane, it was warm and quiet inside.

Lana sat down at the dresser beside the window and dug about in the drawer for the postcards she had bought earlier that day, pointedly ignoring Adam as he came in and flopped face down on to his bed.

'Well, we missed out on pudding.' Adam rolled on to his back and gazed up at the ceiling.

Lana flipped through her postcards, trying to

pick her favourite. 'Yes,' she said. 'Thanks to you.'

'I didn't do anything!' Adam let out another sigh. 'I think it might have been a poltergeist.'

'It might have been a lot of things,' replied Lana.

'I'm serious. I heard it laughing. And I –' Adam didn't know quite how to describe the eerie cold feeling that had accompanied the laughter – 'I felt it.'

'Will you just shut up about ghosts for five minutes,' snapped Lana. 'I'm trying to write to Mum and Dad.'

'I pity the postman who's got to deliver letters to Antarctica.'

'They said to write,' Lana reminded him. 'And they said anything would be sure to reach them at their base camp – eventually.'

She watched her brother as he continued to study the ceiling. It was obvious he was still thinking about poltergeists. 'You should write one too. The least you can do is tell them that Uncle Larry's taking good care of us,' she said. 'Since it was you who got us into this mess in the first place,' she added in an undertone.

Uncle Larry had not been their parents' first choice to look after the twins while they were on their expedition. It was Adam who had persuaded them. He was almost as mad about the supernatural as their uncle was, and he desperately wanted to take part in his show. Uncle Larry had always had a soft spot for Adam and hadn't required much persuading.

Now Adam was having a great time, but Lana would much rather have stayed in London with one of her friends' families. Ever since they had joined the *Fright Night* crew, she seemed to spend most of her time getting cold, wet and into trouble. Not her idea of a great summer holiday.

'I'll write one later,' said Adam, reaching for the remote control. Aiming it at the TV, he tapped the power button. The news was on: lots of boring talk about credit cards and mortgages. He sighed and switched channels.

'Oh no,' he said.

Lana glanced up.

'What?' Her face sank at the sight of the screen and she echoed her brother's tone exactly. 'Oh no.'

A handsome dark-haired man was speaking animatedly to camera, his face lit up from below to cast a riot of strange shadows over his features and on the wall behind him. It looked like he was in a church or cathedral. The next second they cut to a shot of him racing down a darkened stairwell, with the camera chasing him. 'I heard noises!' he shouted. 'There's something down here in the crypt! Stay with me!'

Then they flashed up a caption saying 'Coming Up Next On *Ghosts Unlimited*' and jumped to a shaky shot of a glowing figure hovering in a gloomy archway. It seemed to float towards the camera and the camera got even shakier – then they went to an ad break.

'That is so fake,' said Adam. 'Ghosts don't look like glow-in-the-dark stickers.'

'Well,' retorted Lana, 'it looked pretty good to me. At least they have decent effects on that show. It's better than a lot of nothing – like we find every week.'

'Huh. You sound like Angela. The scariest thing on *Ghosts Unlimited* is that Stuart Smythe. He's not a patch on Uncle Larry.'

'He's pretty slimy,' agreed Lana, thinking of his slick hair and oily smiles.

'Like the spooks in *Ghostbusters*,' Adam laughed. 'I can just see him shaking someone's hand and leaving them covered in ectoplasm.'

Lana shook her head.

'Ecto-what? Actually, I don't want to know.' She

assumed *Ghostbusters* was one of those dumb old films Adam liked to watch. The same sort she liked to avoid. After a pause, she added, 'Do you honestly think Uncle Larry is right? You know, not to use effects and all that. I mean, I love him, and it's clever what he does – he's really good at telling a story and gives a great sense of atmosphere, but . . .' She was almost afraid to go on, knowing how defensive her brother could get. 'Angela does have a point. *Fright Night* has never found a real ghost.'

Adam made a face. 'No, but they wouldn't, would they? Ghosts don't exist, according to you.'

'I never said that,' Lana argued, turning back to her postcard. 'I would just like to see some proof, that's all.'

'Oh, you would, would you? *Hahaha!*'

Lana tutted. 'I think your Irish accent needs some practice.'

She sucked at her pen, and flipped the postcard back over to look at the picture again for inspiration.

'That wasn't my Irish accent,' Adam assured her. 'That wasn't me.'

Lana turned round in her chair. Adam was sitting bolt upright on the bed, his eyes searching the room.

Lana sighed. 'Nice try. About as convincing as Angela's Banshee.'

Adam stared at her. 'I'm not kidding. Honest. I think whatever was playing up at dinner is in here now. Maybe it followed us all the way from the stones!'

Lana wrinkled her brow and pointed her pen threateningly. 'Adam, if you're –'

'*Hahahaha!*' came the laugh again.

Lana's eyes bulged. So did Adam's – but his lips hadn't moved.

'You heard that?' he said.

'I did.' Lana wished she could deny it. She wondered if her brother had started practising ventriloquism.

Lana stood up, struck by an idea. 'I'll bet there's a hole in the wall and someone in the next room is playing games with us!'

Adam jumped up off the bed. It didn't explain the strangeness at dinner, but maybe Lana was right and it was all a practical joke. They got down on all fours and searched along the skirting board, even ferreting under the beds.

Suddenly, from above them came a cold wind and a flapping sound. And a creaking, like somebody jumping up and down on the bed.

'*Woo! Woo!*' the invisible voice wailed.

Adam and Lana stopped what they were doing and looked up.

A figure wrapped in one of the sheets was indeed bouncing on Adam's bed as if it was a trampoline.

'*Woo! Wooooo!*' the sheet-clad figure repeated.

Then, as Adam and Lana watched in disbelief, the sheet fell in a crumpled heap on top of the bed. Revealed before them was the pale, scarcely visible image of a boy. He looked like he had been sketched on the air with deathly white chalk.

'How do you do?' he greeted them politely, as he flashed them a roguish grin. 'The name's Fergus. It's amazing what a ghost has to do to get some attention around here.'

Lana's mouth dropped open.

She imagined she would be a long time closing it again.

4

'Oh, wow,' said Adam. '*Wow!*'

'Wait, so . . . wait,' said Lana. Being lost for words was an unusual sensation for her, and she didn't much like it. She kept staring straight at the boy – and through him. 'You're a real ghost.' It seemed worth stating the obvious when the obvious was so hard to believe.

'I'm afraid so.' The boy, Fergus, stood on the bed – or possibly hovered just above it. He scratched at his spectral hair and fidgeted shiftily, as though he felt a bit shy at being studied so thoroughly.

'I'm Adam Craddock,' Adam chuckled, 'and this is my sister, Lana. She said she wanted proof that ghosts exist, but she's still having trouble believing it, even now the evidence is right in front of her eyes.'

'That's unfair,' replied Lana. 'It takes time to take in something like this.'

'Ah, she's right,' agreed Fergus. 'Took me a while to realize I was a ghost. In fact, it only really started to sink in when I started to sink into things.'

As if to demonstrate, he sank slowly up to his knees into the bed. 'Like that.' He grinned.

'A ghost with a sense of humour. This is brilliant!' said Adam excitedly.

There was still the chill in the air he had felt before, but none of that mattered now as far as he was concerned. He felt like reaching out and putting his hand through the spectre, but he was sure Fergus would think that very rude of him.

'It's amazing,' nodded Lana, gradually taking in the reality of it all. Fergus was little more than a white shadow, but she could tell he was a fair-haired lad, probably about her age, and he was dressed like a street urchin out of some Dickensian drama on TV. But he was definitely here, right before them in their room.

'No, I mean brilliant,' said Adam, struck by a brainwave. 'We can take him to show Uncle Larry. His first real ghost! He'll be over the moon!'

Fergus raised his hands and backed away, gravely serious all of a sudden.

'Oh, no way! He can be over the moon or the sun. And he can be tickled pink and any other colour of the rainbow he cares for, but I'm not going to appear in front of anyone else. I didn't come here to show myself about. I came here to hide.'

Adam gaped, startled by Fergus's abrupt change of mood. 'But —'

'Hide?' asked Lana. 'Hide from what?'

Fergus leaned forward and lowered his voice. 'Well now, brace yourselves for another shock. A witch,' he announced, his face turning paler – if that was possible.

'You're kidding!' Adam's face lit up. 'That's even better. *Fright Night* will have a field day. A ghost and a witch. It'll be Uncle Larry's best episode ever!'

'Hang on, Adam,' Lana said. Then she shook her head and narrowed her eyes at Fergus. There could be no doubting he was a ghost, but that was no reason to believe everything he said. 'First of all, if you're so anxious to hide, why were you messing about down at the dinner table? I mean, that was you, right?'

Fergus floated over to Lana's bed and bounced up and down a bit. 'There's no fooling you, is there, miss? Yes, that was me. I can't help myself. It's my nature. My mum was always giving me a clip round the ear for it too.'

Lana remembered that times were tougher back when Fergus would have been alive. Clips round the ear were probably the least of the punishments dished out to troublesome children. Still, it was difficult to think of this see-through image as ever having been a real boy – it was difficult enough to think of him as a real ghost.

'Well, it was annoying.'

'But I wanted to get your attention. And to shut that bossy woman up.' Fergus giggled and flopped back on the bed. Then he had a go at making a serious face. But he had the sort of cheeky features that made serious faces quite a challenge for him. 'To be fair though, I've been cooped up in those stones for I don't know how long. I had to stretch my game legs and all that.'

'The stones,' said Adam. 'So it was you I heard up there.'

'Sure. You see, I managed to give that witch the slip once before, but those stones just sucked me in. Your old uncle was right about that. Like a great big magnet to us ghosts, they are. Or a whirlpool.'

'And we released you?' asked Lana. 'How?'

'You gave me a way out. When you touched the stone. The stones are like a prison and when a mortal touches one, well, that gives us ghosts a sort of channel into the mortal world. Don't ask me about how it works, though. Haven't the foggiest. But the fact that you're twins and you touched a stone together may have helped. Very powerful, twins are.'

'You could tell we were twins? I mean, from inside the stone?'

'It's hard to explain, but I could *feel* things from in there. The important thing is, I'm free now, thanks to you two. But I really need your help.'

'Because you're being chased by a witch?' said Lana dubiously. Despite her difficulty in dealing with the fact that she was talking with a ghost, she hadn't overlooked that small detail.

'It's the truth!' insisted Fergus, sitting bolt upright. 'And I wasn't the only one to follow you from the stones!' Suddenly, he whizzed over to the window, whipping through Adam and Lana like a breeze and leaving them horribly chilled, as though they had both stepped into a huge freezer. He drew the curtain open a little – and backed away almost instantly. 'She's out there right now!'

Fergus retreated to the wall nervously and disappeared halfway into it. 'Take a look for yourselves!'

Adam and Lana went to the window. First a ghost and now a witch. This was a lot to take in – but neither of them could ignore Fergus's obvious fear, or their own curiosity.

Adam flipped the curtain open and they peered out into the rain and the night. At first, they could see nothing. Most of the houses in the street lay in darkness, and the street lamps on the far pavement were spaced far apart. But then, in the gap between two lamps, right where the shadows were at their deepest, they saw something move.

It was a figure – a woman. She wore a long cloak with a hood drawn over her head to shield herself against the weather, or perhaps to hide herself from prying eyes. Adam leaned forward and opened the curtain wider as he strained for a better look at her.

At the same moment, the woman raised her head sharply and Adam and Lana caught a glimpse of a pale face that seemed to look straight up at the twins.

'Woah!' cried Adam, jumping back from the window as if he'd been burned. Even Lana couldn't stop herself ducking – it felt as if the woman's piercing eyes had gone right through her.

'It could be someone quite innocent – one of the locals out for a walk.'

'Don't be stupid,' replied Adam. 'In this weather? And she knew exactly where we were – she looked straight at us!'

'So what? She looked up at a window. She probably saw the light when you drew the curtain back.'

'Hmm,' said Adam, far from convinced. 'If you're so sure, why don't you take another look.'

Lana had to admit that she felt strangely reluctant to go back to the window. But she refused to let Adam make her look silly, so she peeped through the curtains again.

'See, she's going now.'

Adam came up behind his sister to check for himself.

It was true, the woman was carrying on down the street. She wasn't hunched over, the way Adam imagined a witch should be. All the same, there was something not quite right about her. With a jolt, he realized that most normal people *would* have been huddled over in the face of the wind and the rain. But the strange woman walked straight and tall, as if entirely untroubled by the weather.

'Is she gone?' asked Fergus.

'Yes,' Adam confirmed, as the woman seemed to be swallowed up by the night and the storm.

Fergus stepped fully out of the wall at last. 'Take it from me, she's not innocent. She's a witch. Her name is Ghian and she's as dangerous as witches come.'

'I believe you,' said Adam.

'There's a surprise,' said Lana, with a sigh. 'Well, whoever she is, she's gone on her way.' She glanced at her watch and then at her unfinished postcard on the dresser. Fergus's appearance had disrupted her plans for the evening – not to say turned her world upside down. She suspected she was going to have a lot more to write to Mum and Dad about, but first of all she needed some time to think.

'But she'll be back soon enough. You have to help me,' Fergus urged them both.

'How?' asked Lana.

'I bet Uncle Larry knows how to deal with a witch,' said Adam. 'We could go and ask him about it.'

'But not now,' replied Lana. 'It's really late and Angela doesn't want to see us until the morning, remember? I don't fancy getting caught out of our room trying to find him. We should get some sleep and talk to him first thing tomorrow.'

'Sleep?!' exclaimed Adam. 'Are you kidding? I want to find out more about Fergus.' He turned to the ghost, questions bubbling out of him like fizzy drink from a bottle that had been given a great big shake. 'So we know you can walk into walls and things, and move objects around, right? What else can you do? Can you levitate? What was it like being imprisoned in the stones? How long were you in there for?'

'Adam,' Lana broke in. 'I know *you* could happily stay up all night talking to Fergus. But *I* need some time to get my head around the fact that we've just met a ghost.' She looked at Fergus. 'No offence,' she added.

'Ah, none taken, miss.' He smiled.

'Well, then *you* can go to sleep,' Adam told Lana, 'but me and Fergus are staying up to talk.'

'Adam . . .' Lana was just about to reproach her brother when a flash of lightning lit up the room and a rumble of thunder shook the building.

The lights went out.

Lana looked around. Fergus was a faintly glowing figure painted on the darkness, but she couldn't make out her brother at all. The guest house had fallen eerily silent, and even the storm outside had quietened, as though it had spent all its anger in that last outburst.

'Oh no,' said Fergus.

'What is it?' asked Adam.

'She's here. This is her doing.'

'Don't be silly. It's just a power cut because of the storm.'

'But –'

Adam was interrupted by a noise out in the corridor. A clinking, rattling sound. It was so unexpected, even Lana started. She sighed again, annoyed at herself. Between them, with all their fretting, Adam and Fergus had managed to scare her. It was silly.

'Listen,' said Adam.

Lana listened. At first there was only silence. Then a floorboard creaked, and they heard the slow footsteps of someone coming along the landing. The clink and rattle grew louder. It sounded like someone was shaking a piggy bank full of coins.

Clink and rattle. Rattle and clink. And the stealthy footsteps, louder and nearer. Coming to a halt right outside their door.

Fergus faded to a pale shadow and shrank back against the window, trembling.

Lana was having trouble breathing. *This is ridiculous*, she thought. Adam grabbed hold of her hand.

'It's probably just one of the guests,' she whispered. 'Or Mrs Flanaghan checking on the lights.'

'Carrying a jar of marbles?' hissed Adam. 'Come on, Lana. It's the witch. Has to be. You could at least recognize something supernatural when it's right under your –'

'It's her, sure enough,' hissed Fergus desperately. 'I can't stay here!'

'What? No!' said Adam, trying to shout and whisper at the same time.

There was another clink and rattle. Then, through the gloom, they saw the door handle slowly start to turn . . .

'That's it!' moaned Fergus. 'I'm off!'

'Fergus! *No!*' Adam tried to grab hold of the ghost, but his hands passed straight through him. Fergus whirled around and hurled himself through the window.

Adam and Lana automatically threw their hands up to shield themselves, but of course the glass didn't shatter – Fergus passed clean through and out into the night.

Adam stood there staring out at the storm for a split second. Suddenly he spun round and charged at the door, pushing against it with all his weight to keep it closed.

'He's gone!' he shouted. 'He's not here any more!'

'*Adam!*' hissed Lana.

There was a pause that stretched into a lifetime. Then, slowly, came the sound of footsteps heading away down the landing – and a final clink and rattle, like a note of farewell.

5

By morning, Fergus still hadn't returned. He wasn't under either of the beds or in the wardrobe, and if he was hiding in the walls, there was no coaxing him out.

It had been a long night. After Fergus had gone, Lana had spent hours pretending to sleep, while her thoughts went round and round endlessly in her head. Adam stayed at the window, peering out in the hope of glimpsing Fergus. Later, Lana had rolled over and opened her eyes to see Adam in bed, but sitting up, obviously turning over the evening's events in his own mind.

Eventually, Adam and Lana had both fallen asleep. They woke up with the sun streaming in through their window and a shared disappointment at Fergus's absence. During the night, Lana had even wondered whether she might have imagined the boy ghost, but she couldn't argue with the fact that she had seen him with her own eyes. And since ghosts were now an undeniable fact, Fergus was an exciting find, to say the least. Even so, her disappointment was nothing to her brother's.

Adam threw up his arms and kicked the foot of the bed. 'We can't have lost him already. We can't have!'

'Adam, calm down. Maybe,' suggested Lana, 'he can't appear in the daytime.'

'What, one night with a ghost and you're an expert now?' Adam scoffed.

'Maybe he's having a lie-in in the spirit world,' she continued, trying to cheer her brother up.

'It's serious, Lana.' Adam clenched his teeth anxiously. 'Ghian could have cornered him somewhere. She could have caught him already.'

'But we can't even be sure his witch story is true,' said Lana.

Adam glared at her.

'There's no sense in worrying unnecessarily,' she added quickly, trying not to be too dismissive of her brother's fears. 'That's all I'm saying.'

'Well, we should go and talk to Uncle Larry, right?'

'I'm not sure. Perhaps we should check out Fergus's story for ourselves before we involve Uncle Larry.'

'He's probably going to be busy anyway,' Adam decided, taking a liking to the plan. 'And we can look for Fergus at the same time.'

Agreed, they dressed and headed downstairs. Everything was quiet. In the dining room a waitress was clearing away some breakfast things and only one table was occupied – by Steve, the props man.

Steve looked up from his work and gave them a wave. 'Hello,' he said. 'You're a bit late, aren't you? The rest of the mob went out to make an early start.'

Adam and Lana wandered over. They could see he had the Banshee spread out on the tablecloth in front of him, like a patient on an operating table. Perhaps Steve was hoping to cure it of 'looking like a rubber chicken' disease.

'Didn't Uncle Larry say not to bother with that?' asked Lana.

'Ah.' Steve tapped the side of his nose. 'Angela's orders. Mum's the word. Although I'm glad Angela's not my mum,' he laughed gruffly. 'But I've still got to do what she says, more's the pity.'

'Uncle Larry will be jumping mad,' Adam warned him.

'Well, no offence, but your Uncle Larry's not half so scary, and it's Angela that pays my wages.

Anyway, we might not have to use this if some proper ghosts turn up, so there's no sense in upsetting Larry for no good reason, now is there?'

'I guess not,' said Adam uncertainly. He exchanged a glance with his sister.

'So, do they need us for the shoot today?' asked Lana.

'Don't think so. They're just doing some establishing shots around town. Then they're down at the seafront for the afternoon, to do a piece on some ghost that's supposed to walk up and down the promenade. Angela seemed happy to do without you.'

'Good,' grinned Adam and turned to go.

'Wait up,' said Steve, surprised. 'You're normally hanging around on set for every single shot, whether you're in it or not. What are you up to?'

'What's it to you?' said Adam, a little on the defensive because he didn't have a good story ready.

'We're just going to explore the town,' cut in Lana smoothly. 'We'll be fine. We can take care of ourselves.' She dug out her mobile phone from her pocket and waved it at him. 'And if we get into any trouble, we can call.'

Steve shrugged. 'Hey, fair enough. Best not go

calling your uncle in the middle of a shoot, though.'

'True.' Lana didn't have to imagine Angela's reaction if they interrupted her precious schedule. 'Well, in an emergency, we can always phone you here and you can give him a message,' she said smartly.

'Yeah, like I haven't got enough to do.' Steve gestured at the injured Banshee. 'Go on,' he said, with a wink, 'get out of here.'

Smiling at the waitress as they passed, Adam and Lana grabbed some rolls from the bread basket on the sideboard.

Outside, the skies were grey and overcast but the air was fresh and still, as though taking a much-needed breather between storms. They glanced at the spot where the mysterious woman had stood last night. An ordinary stretch of pavement, it now seemed permanently haunted by the memory of her – even in daylight. It gave the twins a faint sense of uneasiness as they passed.

'Where to first?' said Lana. 'We need to find some sort of proof to support Fergus's witch story.'

'The stones, I suppose,' decided Adam. 'Everything leads there.'

Adam and Lana had been on a tour of the

town with Uncle Larry when they had first arrived in Bray, so they knew the way to the public footpath that led to the stones. They walked down two streets: one that was mostly big Georgian guest houses like Mrs Flanaghan's, the other a row of snug-looking cottages. At the end of the row, they paused to cross the road to an old wooden stile set in a drystone wall.

Adam took his sister's hand and they stepped up to the kerb. They looked left, but there was no traffic coming. They looked right – the road was still clear. They looked left again.

Which was when, from a narrow lane between the cottages, something large and black jumped out at them.

6

Lana screamed. The black shape flew through the air straight towards them – and doubled up with a dose of the giggles.

It was Fergus, of course – there was no mistaking the voice or the breath of cold air that accompanied it. Apparently he could appear in the daytime after all, when or if he chose to. And at the moment he seemed to have chosen to appear wrapped in a black bin bag.

Recovering from his laughter, he cast away the bin bag as though a sudden gust of wind had simply blown it off him. There he stood, as ghost-like and see-through as he had been last night. It was a wonder a light breeze didn't take him away.

Lana met his grin with a stern scowl. 'What do you think you're doing, scaring us like that?'

'Scaring's one of the things I'm best at. I tell

you, those newfangled bags are as good as sheets. And black stands out better in the day. But it still takes practice to get a good scream!'

'You might want to practise on someone else. I thought you wanted our help.'

'Sure. Against the witch. But you can't help with the pranks. I told you, I can't help it *myself*.'

'Like you can't help making us feel cold?' Adam made a show of shivering, but it wasn't entirely an act.

'Exactly,' said Fergus. 'It's just the way I am.'

'You could try growing up,' said Lana.

Fergus looked suddenly wounded, averting his gaze and clasping a hand to his chest. 'Aw now, miss, that's the one thing I can't ever do.'

He turned and drifted off a little way, head bowed low.

As she watched him go, Lana realized that she and Adam had quite overlooked what must have happened to Fergus to make him become a ghost. They'd been so amazed at seeing and speaking to a ghost that they'd forgotten he must have died very young. 'I'm sorry,' she said, following him, 'I didn't mean to –'

Adam caught up with her and grabbed her sleeve. 'He's having you on, Lana.'

She looked at Adam, frowning. 'Shh!' she said.

But when she turned back to Fergus, he was wearing another wicked grin. 'That,' she scowled, 'is mean. We should leave you to the witch.'

'Oh now, don't be hasty, miss,' said Fergus, quickly. 'We could make a good team, you, your brother and me.'

'Huh! That's all very well, but I think you ought to know – Adam was worried about you. Running off like that. He thought Ghian might have caught you.'

'It's true,' Adam admitted. 'It was just a nasty thought, but –'

'And what about you, miss? Didn't you worry about me too?'

'A little,' admitted Lana grudgingly.

Fergus laid a hand on his chest again, this time with a shy smile. 'I'm touched you'd both care enough to worry about me. But I had to keep clear of Ghian. You have to understand that.'

'Hmm,' considered Lana. He wasn't the only one who could play games. 'But you could have come back later. If you worry my brother like that again,' she warned severely, 'we'll hand you over to that witch in a flash.'

Fergus gulped and looked horrified. 'You wouldn't do that, miss.'

'Now she's having *you* on,' Adam told Fergus

– although a glance at his sister told him she was at least half serious. 'But if we're going to check out this witch of yours, where do we start looking for her? Up at the stones?'

Fergus nodded, indicating the far end of the street. 'Absolutely. While I was keeping myself out of sight this morning, I saw her heading out of town. I reckon she's off to the cliffs and very likely the stones. Like I said, her lair's somewhere nearby and she's always rambling about up there. We should go and take a look – you'll soon see that she's a witch, sure enough.'

'All right then,' decided Adam. 'What are we waiting for?'

'But, Fergus, won't it be dangerous for you?' asked Lana. 'Going near the stones? Couldn't you get sucked back into them?'

'We'll have to be careful. But we needn't go too near.' The ghost cracked a big smile. 'Besides, now I've got you two with me, you can always release me again.' And with that he set off ahead of them.

'Well, we might have to think twice about that,' muttered Lana as they hurried after. Just as the ghost couldn't help making mischief, she couldn't help having her doubts. Considering that he had been trapped inside them, Fergus seemed very keen to go back to the stones. Part of her wondered if he had some secret reason for wanting to lead them there. He certainly didn't seem nearly as terrified as he had been the night before.

'Adam,' she hissed, keeping her voice low and hoping that Fergus didn't have supernaturally sharp hearing, 'how do we know he's telling the truth?'

'What do you mean?'

'Well, we've only got his word for it that he was trapped in the stones. What if he didn't "escape" at all – what if he's working for the witch?'

'Listen to you! "Working for the witch." Yesterday, you didn't even believe in witches. Besides, why would he try to trick us?'

'I don't know. But that's just it – we don't really know anything about him.'

'Why do you have to be so suspicious?' asked Adam in exasperation. 'He's friendly, isn't he? And he was really scared of the witch last night. He's obviously a good ghost. Now come on.'

Lana frowned as Adam strode off after Fergus. Her brother might have made up his mind that Fergus was on the level, but she certainly hadn't. Lana quickened her pace. She had a few questions for their transparent 'friend' . . .

*

There was something eerie about the cliff tops – their exposed slopes of long grass and scattered rocky outcrops gave them a wild appearance even in calm weather. The crash of waves below was fairly gentle, but there was a sense that the sea had only been temporarily tamed, and the horizon was already misting over with a promise of fog, or worse.

The path was muddy, puddled with rainwater and very uneven – and a lot more uphill than down. Adam and Lana were puffing after the first couple of rises. Fergus, of course, had no such problems.

Adam watched him moving ahead with his jaunty stride, and marvelled at the way his feet often barely grazed the ground – evidence that he was actually floating along and only pretending to walk.

'So, Fergus,' Adam asked, 'how is it you can sink into the bed and hide in the walls and stuff – but other times you can touch things, pick up things and throw them around?'

Fergus about-faced and floated backwards for a while. 'Ah, that'll be because I'm made up of energy. It's a question of how I focus it.' Making a show of concentration, he gradually became more solid, as though colouring himself in with a white pen. There was still a suggestion of lightness about him, but now it was as if he was made of cloud or snow, instead of watery paint and faint shadow. 'The closer we get to the stones, the harder that's going to be. It's going to take most of my concentration just keeping myself from getting sucked back into them.'

'So, what's it like – being a ghost?' asked Lana, trying not to sound too suspicious. 'If you don't mind me asking.'

'Well, it was fun to begin with.' Then Fergus made a face. 'Leastways, until I was dragged off.'

'Into the stones?'

'Well, not right away, worse luck. Ghian was waiting for me.'

'How d'you mean, "waiting for you"?' asked Lana, with a meaningful look at Adam.

'Well, I'm a homeless ghost. I was roaming the streets down in Cork, where I was born and raised. See, I figured I couldn't go back home, after I – you know,' the lad explained. 'My mum would be too upset to see me and all. So after a while, I settled on the local bakery and I spent a few decades there. Scaring folks and making them drop cakes and buns and things.' He gave a sigh. 'Even though they weren't much use to me, I sure liked all the smells.' He gave a dreamy smile and appeared to breathe in deeply. 'Mmm.'

'*Decades?*' Lana couldn't believe how casually he referred to tens of years.

'Sure, you've a lot of time on your hands when you're a ghost. Anyway, I'd always felt something giving me a little tug, like the moon pulls at the tide, I suppose. Eventually, I thought I'd follow it and see what it was. Well, it led here – to Bray. The tugging was even stronger here, but I managed to hang about in the town for a while. They had a nice bakery here too, you know. But it got harder and harder to resist that pull. Then, one day I was walking along, minding my own business, when *whoosh!* this tremendous force takes hold of me and I'm dragged off like I'm in a raging river or something.'

'Ley lines!' cried Adam.

'What lines?' replied Lana.

'You remember – Uncle Larry mentioned them last night. Lines of energy that lie across the whole world, connecting magical sites. The Shrieking Stones stand at a point where ley lines meet. It must be the ley lines that pull the ghosts in.'

'Whatever,' sniffed Fergus. 'It wasn't a pleasant feeling. And it was a whole lot less pleasant when, instead of being sucked into the stones, I was nabbed by Ghian. She trapped me like a butterfly. Used a bottle instead of a net, but still.'

'A bottle?' Adam was reminded of the genie in the lamp.

'She had some terrible magic in there. Chippings from the stones, I think they were. That's what you heard her rattling last night. They dragged me in, as sure as the stones themselves would have done if she hadn't been waiting for me.' Fergus gave a shudder, which set his ghostly image rippling in the air. Then he gave one of his broad grins. 'Lucky thing is, if you ever find yourself trapped in a bottle, it's pretty easy to break once you learn how to topple yourself off the shelf.'

'Sounds like a simple escape,' mused Lana. *But I wonder if it was as simple as he says*, she thought.

'Ha! Yes, it was, miss. Except I came out too close to those stones and got sucked straight into them. And there I stayed, for another whole lot of decades.' Fergus smiled thinly, as if he wanted to put that memory behind him. 'But now I'm free again – free to have some more fun and learn some more tricks of the trade, so to speak. See, there's a difference between being a ghost and knowing exactly how it all ticks. You pick things up by experience. It's like when you've got hiccups. I'll bet you know a half-dozen ways to cure them, but I'm sure you don't know how any of them works.'

'Well, if either of us gets hiccups,' said Adam, 'we'll just call on you to give us a fright.'

'Ha ha!' Apparently Fergus liked that idea. 'I'll be happy to be of service.'

Suddenly, though, the smile fell from Fergus's face and he sank down into the earth. Instinctively, Adam and Lana ducked too.

'There she is!' whispered Fergus urgently, pointing. 'Ghian!'

They followed his outstretched finger. Indeed, there was someone – a woman, hooded and cloaked – picking her way along the brow of a hill. One glance this way and whoever she was couldn't fail to spot the trio.

Adam and Lana tensed, crouching low and keeping themselves perfectly still. Fergus sank further into the ground, until only his head poked out.

'It's the woman from last night,' agreed Adam.

'There can't be many people around here who dress like that,' Lana had to admit. 'Can't we just go up and talk to her?' After last night's scare, she was far from keen on the idea, but she wasn't prepared to admit that in front of her brother.

'No way,' protested Fergus. 'She'd have us all for breakfast.'

'Let's just follow her for a bit,' suggested Adam. 'See what she's up to and where she goes.'

'All right,' said Lana reluctantly. She preferred to deal with people honestly and upfront. All this sneaking around could land them in trouble – even if the woman was only an eccentric local, she probably wouldn't take kindly to being spied on by two children and a ghost. Together, they rose carefully and set off in pursuit.

The witch, if that was truly what she was, was a fast walker and they had to move quickly, ducking down whenever it looked like she might glance back. She never did, though, and they managed to keep her in sight until she crested a hill and disappeared down the other side.

With the woman out of sight, they ran quickly up the hill themselves, hoping to make up some ground. But when they reached the ridge and peered over, Adam was surprised to see that she was still well ahead of them, striding along the cliff edge. Ahead of her was the familiar granite circle of the Shrieking Stones, standing watch over this stretch of the coast. The mist they had noticed earlier was moving in and lending the stones a touch of their customary eeriness.

Adam, Lana and Fergus walked briskly on, keeping an eye on the fast-moving figure.

'She might stop at the stones,' warned Lana.

'Yeah, we'll have to be careful she doesn't spot us then.'

'Trust me, careful is my middle name when it comes to Ghian,' Fergus assured them.

By the time they neared the stones, the mist was steadily thickening into a fog. If not yet soupy, the air had become a cloudy broth in a surprisingly short space of time. Just as Fergus had warned, he was becoming harder to see, his outline fading as the fog grew murkier.

The woman did not stop at the stones, but marched straight through the mighty circle.

'We can't go that way,' said Fergus; 'I'd be sucked in, for sure.'

'Don't worry,' replied Adam, 'we'll go round.'

So Adam led his companions on an inland detour around the stones, keeping Fergus well clear of them. But the delay was costly. When they reached the far side, there was no trace of the woman.

They stopped to search for her, their expressions growing more frustrated by the second. To lose her now would be such a shame.

Suddenly, Lana's sharp eyes made out the cloaked figure again.

'There she is!'

About as far ahead as they could see – which, in the fog, was not all that far – the woman appeared as little more than a dark smudge. She was walking in the shadow of a large rock formation – an enormous stack of flat boulders a little beyond the stones.

'Well done!' Adam congratulated his sister. 'Come on.'

He set off, leading them onward, now just trusting to luck that the woman wouldn't look their way. Then, just as quickly, they all stopped.

'Where'd she go?' said Adam.

Lana narrowed her eyes. The smudge of a figure had faded to nothing. 'She just – vanished!'

'Aye,' said Fergus, gazing around at the murky atmosphere. 'Into thick air.'

7

They quickened their pace. The fog was spilling in over the cliffs to steal away the daylight. Heavy and grey, it was closing in thick and a good deal too fast, as though the weather was helping the mysterious woman to cover her tracks.

'This is a mite spooky,' muttered Fergus.

'You ought to know,' complained Lana. Like her brother, she was having to watch her footing on the lumpy ground. She glanced back, to make sure the gnarled pillars of the Shrieking Stones were still visible. There they stood all right, set against the fast-disappearing shadow of cliff-edge and looking graver than ever – like the fingers of some granite giant reaching out of the ground. But they would be the only real landmark when it came to finding their way back, and they were already vanishing in the swirling mist. Lana's feelings of unease were getting stronger. The woman could be lurking anywhere. What if Fergus had led them into a trap?

'Down here!' Adam whispered forcefully, tugging on Lana's sleeve.

They had arrived at the stack of flat rocks where they had last seen the woman. What had seemed like a single rock formation was actually a pair, standing very close together. Here the ground dropped away into a cleft, an earthen path descending into the gap between the two. It was fairly narrow, but certainly wide enough for a person.

Fergus nodded. 'It'll be her cave. Where she does all her evil work.'

'"Evil work",' Lana scoffed. 'Come on, we can't even be sure she's a witch.'

'Yeah?' replied Adam. 'Why are you whispering then?'

'All right, it's – a bit suspicious,' admitted Lana, deliberately raising her voice a little. 'I mean, her being out here. In this weather. But she could just be the outdoor type. She could be collecting wild flowers or –'

'That she might be,' Fergus interrupted, 'for potions and such.'

'Fergus wouldn't lie to us.' Adam was keen to demonstrate his trust in his new friend, but then again, it couldn't hurt to ask: 'Would you, Fergus?'

He looked around for confirmation, but although they were at a safe distance from the stones, Fergus still appeared to be having trouble staying visible. He just hung there as though he had been painted on the air.

Lana wasn't so sure, and was not afraid to show it. 'No, he just likes to play pranks and give people scares. And anyway, don't forget where – or when – Fergus is from. Back then, any woman who acted a bit oddly was called a witch.'

'Trust me, I am not playing a joke,' protested Fergus. 'Not this time. You can go down there and see for yourselves. But you be careful, that's all.'

Adam frowned. 'You're not coming with us?'

Fergus shook his see-through head. 'No, thanks.'

'Oh no, no way!' said Lana. 'If we're going into a witch's den, you're coming with us.'

Fergus backed away from Lana's glare, fading further away until he was tissue-paper thin. 'Begging your pardon, miss, but you took the words right out of my mouth. No way.'

'Come on, Fergus,' said Adam. 'I thought we were a team.'

'What are you afraid of anyway? You're a ghost. You're already –'

'Don't say it, miss. It's an ugly word – and those of us that *are* don't especially wish to *hear* it.' Fergus solidified a little so as to give Lana his best black look. 'You don't know anything about what it's like. The stones are really pulling at me – it's taking all my strength just to fight them. I wouldn't be any use to you. And I'm telling you, sure as I'm Fergus, that lady is a witch and she has her ways. She can do worse things to me now than she could have done to me when I was alive. I'm not going down there.'

'But we'll be OK?' asked Adam.

'Just don't let her see you.'

Adam looked at Lana. She shook her head. 'I don't like it, Adam. Whether she's a witch or not.'

'I know.' Adam shrugged. 'But how are we going to find out if we don't take a look? And imagine what it'll do for the show if she *is* a witch.'

Lana rolled her eyes. 'Yeah, because she's really going to want to be on TV.'

Deep down, Lana had known there would be no backing out – even if Fergus had genuine reasons for his reluctance, she and her brother were definitely a team.

'You stay right there, Fergus. If we need you, we'll call you.'

Lana turned in Fergus's direction as she spoke, but the boy had disappeared completely. Lana's insides tightened.

'Adam – Fergus has gone . . .' she began. But her brother was already halfway down the path to the cleft. Gritting her teeth, she followed him.

Down at the base of the cleft, a dark crack opened up. Like a narrow mouth with parched lips, it seemed to blow a chill breath in their faces. Adam knew it was the cold air whipping about in the confined spaces between the rocks. But even so, he felt an urge to take his sister's hand as they took their first cautious steps into the darkness.

The ground was uneven and covered with rocks that did their best to trip the twins, but the path gradually became clearer, eventually turning into a carved staircase as it wound round and down into the earth. Adam wished he had thought to bring a torch. Instead, he and his sister had to feel their way, probing with their feet and hands, until the gloom gave way to dimly wavering light playing over the rock wall.

Finally, round the very next corner, the twins

reached the bottom of the stairs, and a cavern lit up with a flickering orange glow. Peering out from the shadows of the doorway, they could just make out most of the large cave – and what they saw took their breath away.

Candles of all sizes – short and fat, tall and spindly – perched around the walls, dribbling wax down over the rock as they struggled to illuminate the chamber and all its mysterious treasures. In the centre was an arrangement of wooden benches and flat rocks. They may have been altars but, alongside the great bronze, bubbling cauldron hanging over a wood fire and the clutter of bowls and other items nearby, they looked strangely like kitchen worktops. Books lay open everywhere and there were others on shelves, next to jars of herbs, spices, unidentifiable powders and liquids, and other unpleasant things, their shapes constantly shifting in the flickering candlelight, but some of which seemed to stare out through the glass with wide eyes. On one stretch of wall hung a tapestry, unfinished at one end, suspended across a small gap – a bit like a hammock – to connect to a rickety old loom. The woman they had followed was nowhere to be seen.

Lana produced her mobile phone. 'I suppose we should try to take a picture,' she whispered, her expression gloomy. 'It probably won't come out.' She knew the phone's camera wasn't up to much. It didn't have a flash and, even with all the candles, the cavern was very dark.

'Well, it's worth a try.' Adam was annoyed with himself for having left his own phone back in their room. 'This is too good an opportunity to miss.'

Lana took a couple of shots before putting her phone away. 'It does look like a witch's den,' she admitted. 'Or lair. Do witches have dens or lairs?' Her voice was the barest whisper, but it still seemed to carry too far, and many of the candle flames stirred, as though excited at the prospect of visitors.

'More importantly,' answered Adam, 'where's the witch?'

'Maybe there are other rooms. She'd need somewhere to sleep,' Lana pointed out, 'and, well, a toilet.'

Adam stifled a laugh. Trust Lana to think of practicalities at a time like this! 'We could take a look around, but I think we've seen enough. I don't fancy finding a witch's toilet, let alone running into her.'

'Oh, but you can't be thinking of leaving already, children?'

Silently, the woman they had been following glided out of the shadows on the far side of the cavern.

She threw back her black hood, revealing a pale face and long tangles of red hair that looked as if she brushed it regularly with a bramble bush. Under her cloak she wore a gown of browns and greens, decorated with golden symbols that glimmered in the candlelight.

'You must be cold,' she said. 'What would you say to a nice hot bowl of soup?'

'N-no,' managed Adam.

'Thank you,' added Lana. 'We really should be on our way.'

They turned to go.

And there she was, looming over them on the stairs.

Adam and Lana gasped and both automatically glanced back over their shoulders, to where the first woman calmly stood.

The woman on the stairs clicked her fingers and the first one vanished.

Adam and Lana stared, their mouths open to speak, but the woman interrupted.

'But – but – but – but –' she mocked. 'That's what you want to say, isn't it? Those are the words bursting to come out of you right now!' The woman chuckled darkly. 'You've been following a phantom, pursuing a projection, shadowing a shadow!' She cackled, and her raucous laughter echoed round the cavern, sounding far too old to have come from such a young-looking woman. Up close, they could see her complexion was smooth like eggshell and her hair looked to have a few thorny twigs in it, possibly confirming the bramble-bush theory. 'Yes, and now it's landed you in a deep well of trouble! So what would you say to that soup now, eh? *Eh?!*'

And the witch grabbed them by their collars – leaving them no choice in the matter.

8

The witch kept a firm grasp on Adam and Lana as she marched them into the centre of the cavern. Together, they glanced warily at the cauldron, fearful that they were destined to end up *in* the soup.

The witch led them right up to the cauldron and shoved their faces into the heady fumes steaming up from the simmering liquid. It smelt of a variety of different flowers, their scents clashing powerfully, but it was a lot murkier than any soup Adam and Lana had ever seen, and there were earthier, far less pleasant smells brewing underneath.

'Yes, let your noses bask in that,' their captor sighed, taking a deep sniff herself. 'Mmm. It's hubbling and bubbling away nicely. And I went to a great deal of toil and trouble over it, believe you me.' She leaned in and poked her head between them, flicking her eyes from Adam to

Lana and back again. 'That's all we witches are to you children, isn't it? Rhymes and Halloween; bat-wings and broomsticks. Well, we're very real, we have busy lives – and we don't care to have children come barging in on us uninvited.'

'But you led us here!' Lana protested.

Adam backed her up. 'Yeah, with that illusion of yourself. You just told us so.'

The witch made a twisted-up face. 'Bah! What if I did. That *boy* would have led you here anyway. I was merely taking charge of matters, making sure things went according to *my* plans and not yours.'

'We didn't have any plans,' said Adam honestly.

'That's right,' said Lana. 'We just wanted to find out about you. Fergus said –'

The witch snatched tighter handfuls of their collars. 'Yes, Fergus. That's the boy. And that's a good idea. We should start with introductions.' She flashed them a thin and fleeting smile. 'I'm Ghian. How do you do? And you're . . .' She tugged roughly at Lana's collar. '. . . Lana, and you're . . .' She tugged at Adam's. '. . . Adam. There, now that's good manners.'

Lana frowned. 'How do you know our names? Did Fergus tell you?'

'She's been spying on us,' Adam accused angrily. He didn't care for this witch manhandling them like this.

'Spying is rude. Watching over you is what I'd call it. Yes, that's a much nicer way of putting it. And you need watching over, little dears, believe me. You two have unleashed a dangerous little ghost on the world. A spiteful spirit.'

'Fergus? He's not dangerous.'

'All he does is play pranks,' agreed Lana, trying to sound surer than she felt.

'Oh, you think so? Yes, you're children, so of course you know best. Trust me, I'm older than I look and I know a deal better than you. Pranks and games, yes, that's how it starts. Gets him into your good books, appeals to you with his roguish charms. Tells stories too, I'll warrant. But come, I'll show you something.'

Ghian yanked their collars again, pulling them across the cavern. As they went, Adam passed an eye over the contents of her shelves, in the hope of finding out something about the sort of magic this witch practised. Some of the books looked familiar to him from pictures he'd seen in Uncle Larry's library. The jars and bottles were all unlabelled, though, and told him nothing – except that Ghian either was highly disorganized or possessed some supernatural ability when it came to keeping track of their contents. It was like being hurried through a museum of witchcraft by a guide who ought to have been one of the exhibits. In any case, there was no time to study anything before Ghian came to a halt in front of the tapestry that decorated one wall.

'There, look, another story for you. In pictures.'

Seen close up, the true beauty of the tapestry became clear. Embroidered illustrations, made with colourful and intricate threads, were accompanied by words and dates in ornate lettering of green and gold along the top and bottom edges. Each illustration seemed to tell the story of one person – usually a woman – and the one they were looking at right in front of them ended up tied to a stake, standing in a raging inferno of red, orange and yellow stitches. It was a grim subject, but a disturbing amount of care had obviously gone into those flames.

'I saw something like this before,' said Adam. 'In France.'

'That's right,' added Lana. 'Bayeux. Mum and Dad took us. It was all about history – the Norman Conquest and the Battle of Hastings.'

'My, my, such educated, well-travelled children,'

Ghian sighed. 'Well, perhaps my modest efforts can teach you something more.' As Adam and Lana scanned along the cloth, Ghian narrated. 'See, this is about history too – the history of witches. Irish witches. They are all here. But as you can see, many of them lived short lives and met with very unfortunate ends.'

As she spoke, Ghian's lip curled and a bitter tone filled her voice. She shifted her grip to their necks, her fingers stretching all the way round so that her long fingernails danced at their throats. 'Burned at the stake, roasted like mutton, but alive – so you could watch your own skin blacken and smoke. Or drowned on ducking stools, starved of air and bloated with water, jeered by the crowd every time they brought you to the surface to see if you were dead yet. Yes, all because people didn't like magic. All fear and mistrust, they were.'

As they watched, horrified, Adam and Lana saw the embroidered flames flicker – and the face of the woman in the tapestry twisted in agony. Under the whistle of the breeze blowing through the cavern, they were sure they could hear the faint crackle of the fire and the woman's tortured screams.

'Please,' said Lana, 'stop.' She wanted to believe

it was her imagination, but somehow she knew it was something Ghian was doing.

'There's no stopping history, my dear.' The witch tightened her grip on the children's necks, kept their heads facing rigidly forward. 'Just as there's no halting progress. Strange, I gather magic is very popular now, in your films and books and what have you. Pah! It wasn't like that before. No, we witches were made to suffer for our arts and our beliefs. Because we thought differently from other people. That's like you, young Adam, being made to suffer because you prefer chips to mashed potatoes.'

Adam wasn't sure about the comparison, but he kept quiet. It was the best way he could think of to hide the fact that he was trembling.

The witch indicated the section of tapestry next to the one they were facing. 'That part there covers the nineteenth century. You'll see there are far fewer witches being thrown on bonfires or dipped in the drink. And you'd think that was a sign of things improving for us, wouldn't you? But no – it just meant there were hardly any of us left. And those of us there were lived secret, hidden lives, spending every day in fear of being found out. Anyone – anyone – could report us to the Church or to the magistrates, and that would be the end for us. A hot, fiery death – or a cold, choking, wet one. Not much of a choice, was it?'

'No,' said Lana quietly, a lump in her own throat. She was afraid to swallow, with Ghian's fingernails so close to her jugular.

'True,' said Adam. It was difficult to sympathize with this crazy woman, but then again it was difficult to imagine what people accused of being witches must have gone through – all the way back to medieval times. 'But what's all this got to do with Fergus?'

'Ah now,' breathed Ghian, her eyes flaring and her lips forming an even uglier curl. 'That boy is a mean one. Pranks and games it may have been when he was a lad. But as a ghost, he would hunt down witches, bringing mobs knocking on our doors. He roamed all of Ireland, making sure we witches were cooked or ducked and done for.'

'But – why would he do all that?' asked Lana.

Ghian studied them both carefully, as though debating whether to share a dark secret. Slowly, she bent lower to whisper into their ears. 'Here's the thing you should know: naughty children become evil ghosts. They have a mischievous streak, you see, and that's all very well when they're children, but they get very sore at dying so young. And once they're ghosts, that streak grows bigger and nastier and more dangerous.'

'That's crazy,' said Adam. 'Fergus isn't evil.'

'Hmm,' answered Ghian, arching one of her eyebrows. 'And how long have you known him, eh? Known him for years, I have. Decades. Longer. I told you, I'm older than I look, and I'm telling you, that boy is a devil!'

Adam shot Lana a sidelong glance. Although Fergus had expressed a dislike of Ghian, Adam just couldn't imagine the ghost being so bad. But Lana hadn't been so sure, had she? For the first time, Adam felt doubts twist in his stomach. It *was* true that they hadn't known Fergus very long, and Ghian did seem to have a very personal grudge against him. Adam needed to get away from here and think about it all – but first they had to escape from the witch.

'Well, thank you for warning us about Fergus,' he said, 'but we should really be going. Our uncle will be wondering where we are.'

'Yeah,' said Lana, 'but we promise we'll think about what you've said.'

'Oh no, no, no. You must stay,' Ghian insisted cheerily, as she released her grip on their necks and flounced off to one of the shelves to rummage along a row of bottles, making them clink like a glass xylophone. 'You must have soup,' she continued. 'I just need to find another ingredient, in case your little friend turns up. It's his favourite, you see. I put it down somewhere for safekeeping and now it's hidden itself. Ach, it's always the way . . .'

She gave a gentle laugh, a lighter, almost musical version of her usual cackle. 'Aha!' she said, retrieving a bottle of sea-blue glass from behind the others.

Adam took hold of his sister's hand and stood firm. 'Well, thanks, but we really must be off. It's kind of you to offer, but –'

Ghian's mood changed like the weather. She rounded on Adam and Lana so violently that every candle flame trembled and sinister shadows danced across her face. *'You'll do as I say!'* She advanced on them, her features scrunched up fiercely. 'Little children need to respect their elders and do as they're told. Haven't I taught you anything about manners?'

'Hey, witchy! Leave them kids alone!'

Ghian whirled round. It was Fergus's voice, bouncing all around the cavern.

A breath of breeze blew out a line of candles and Fergus chuckled invisibly. A stronger gust whipped along one of the benches, scattering scrolls, setting pages of open books flapping, and hurling bowls and other items aside.

Ghian shook the bottle and it rattled, just like it had done at Mrs Flanaghan's the night before. She popped the cork and waved the bottle about as she advanced through the cavern, stalking like a hunter. 'Come on, boy. You know you can't resist the stones.'

She cackled and that put a stop to Fergus's echoing laughter.

As Adam and Lana watched, jars began to leap off one of the far shelves, one after the other, like glass lemmings. 'Go!' shouted Fergus. 'Adam! Lana! Run!'

'They're not going anywhere! And neither are you, boy – except where Ghian wants you!'

The witch snarled, as more of her things were tossed from shelves and benches. She flitted wildly from one side of the cave to another, waving her bottle all the while, as though trying to get Fergus to catch a whiff of whatever scent was inside.

Adam tugged his sister towards the exit. 'Come on!'

'That's it! Go!' cried Fergus, as a row of jars popped open, spraying the air with different-coloured powders, like dusty fireworks.

The twins dashed across the cavern floor, but

just as they reached the stairs, a desperate cry made them stop and look back. They could see Fergus at last: like a white cloud painted on the dark air, his face was stretched and contorted all out of proportion, and his mouth was drawn impossibly wide as he was sucked into Ghian's bottle like some sort of reverse genie.

Ghian was laughing fit to burst and all but dancing on the spot.

'*Aaaaaaagh!*' cried Fergus, the sound of his scream fading in a warbling spiral, as though he was disappearing down a plughole.

And then his cries were cruelly cut short, as Ghian stopped up the bottle with the cork.

Adam and Lana stared in disbelief. Even in the candlelight, they could see the poor boy's features all squashed up inside the bottle, his face and hands flattened against the inside of the glass.

Ghian found the sight extremely amusing. She wagged a finger at the boy's bulging eyes. 'You know, they say you shouldn't keep things bottled up. But ghosts, they're a different matter!'

Fergus, meanwhile, squeezed-up and bug-eyed, was staring all the way across the cavern at Adam and Lana. With a painful effort, he moved his mouth to shape the word 'Go!'

Ghian tucked the bottle away in a hidden pocket inside her cloak, then turned to grin at the twins. Adam and Lana tore themselves from the sight and bolted up the stairs.

9

The stone staircase was a dark and dizzying spiral and the steps were treacherous, causing the twins to stumble. Every time, they would pick each other up and carry on racing upward.

Behind, they could hear Ghian's scrabbling footsteps chasing them. The witch's voice echoed after them: 'Come here, my little darlings! Come back to Auntie Ghian!'

Adam and Lana could think of half a dozen things they could have shouted back at her, but they said nothing and kept running. The stairs wound up and up – finally – into the open air. But the daylight was so gloomy with fog that breaking out of the cave didn't feel at all like freedom.

Ghian's cackle followed them outside, amplified by the stairs and rebounding off the surrounding rocks.

'Come, come! Too much fresh air will blight your lungs! The weather is cold and rotten – like old fish! You'll catch your deaths!'

Adam glanced back and tensed. There was the witch, coming at them out of the underground darkness, her cloak spreading like bat-wings and her arms reaching out as if to scoop them up in a loving hug.

Lana started up the cleft and Adam scrambled after her. Again they stumbled, scraping their knees, but forced themselves to keep going. Lana reached the top first and turned, throwing her hand out for her brother. He grasped it gratefully and let her pull him up.

Below them, Ghian was making short work of the climb, hopping up the rocky slope like a mad mountain goat.

Now they were on open ground and Adam had to search around for the stones to get his bearings. They were even harder to make out than before, but yes, they were still visible – faintly. Great block-shouldered ogres, shrouded in mist.

But as they raced towards them, Adam couldn't shake off the fear that Ghian would be able to make even better speed once she was free of the rocks.

She did. She practically flew after them.

Lungs burning, Adam and Lana forced themselves into the hardest run of their lives. Floating after them, flitting low over the ground much as Fergus had done, the witch waved her arms in an elaborate pattern, as though she was beckoning to the thick fog.

The twins watched in horror as, around them, swirls of mist began to take on a sinister shape. At first, Adam thought the fog was merely thickening, but soon he could see that dark patches were clumping together like ominous grey candyfloss. Far worse, the clumps sprouted legs and began to scurry this way and that in mid-air, shaping strands of the fog as though it was silk. Fog spiders were spinning misty, silky webs to cut off the twins' escape.

Many of the spiders were tiny, and they worked furiously like a small army of weavers, hanging up their handiwork all around like delicate nets. Three or four others were still forming, gathering in the fog and growing into fat-bodied monsters. These giant fog spiders twitched into horrid life and scuttled across the grass.

They closed in fast on Adam and Lana.

Adam's chest was pounding, but somehow he managed to drag more speed out of his feet – and he kept hold of his sister's hand. As they ran,

Adam scoured the ground for rocks or stones he could fling at the creatures. Bumpy as it was, though, there were no missiles to be had. They were defenceless. All they could do was keep running.

As the webs closed round them, a single silky thread fastened itself to Adam's left hand. It stuck fast and almost pulled Adam back. He yelled out and Lana grabbed hold of him, and it took both of them, together, to yank him free. They ran on.

But on their eight spindly legs of fog, the spiders were faster. One of the monsters was so close, Lana thought she felt one of its forelegs brush the back of her neck.

She screamed and ran harder.

To her horror, though, she still felt the spider's leg tickling over her skin, creeping round the front of her throat. She glanced down – and wished she hadn't. She saw three – no, four – six! – of the miniature spiders crawling on her coat lapels, and suddenly she realized she could feel more of the little creatures scurrying over her neck, stringing their tacky strands of web all over her.

Lana dropped her brother's hand and slapped frantically at herself, swiping at web and spiders alike. But she couldn't run so fast while she was distracted, and the pursuing monster arachnids were closing the gap again.

'Lana, come *on*!'

Adam snatched her hand back and tugged her on, holding his other arm up to shield his face, wiping away a mess of misty cobwebs that had laced itself across his forehead and into his hair.

Behind them, once again, Lana felt the forelegs of the giant spider reach for her. All around them the air was a misty net, crawling with fog spiders of all sizes. Spinning and weaving and fencing off every escape route.

Ahead of them, more of the tiny creatures were spinning furiously away, draping their web right across Adam and Lana's path.

They had one chance: the web hadn't quite reached the ground. Yet.

Adam hurled himself into a desperate dive, pulling his sister after him. Together they hit the damp grass and rolled – under the web.

They tumbled messily down the hill, scrabbling to pick themselves up at the bottom. Glancing back, Lana saw the first of the giant spiders slam noiselessly into the web. Both broke apart in a tangle of smoky swirls.

Ghian's laughter echoed on all sides. If she was disappointed, she wasn't showing it. As they watched, the webs and spiders began to dissolve, being absorbed back into the surrounding fog as their mistress appeared on the crest of the slope.

Adam and Lana took to their heels again, but Ghian showed no signs of pursuit. Instead, she cupped a hand to her mouth, calling after them: 'Fly! Fly, little angels! Don't lose yourselves in the fog now! You'll be needing to find your way when you come back to Auntie Ghian! Soon enough!'

She waved at them as though she was seeing them off on a day trip. Then she blew them a kiss and cackled heartily to herself, watching them run.

'Ha!' puffed Lana, with too little breath left to express the relief she really felt. 'She needn't bet on that.'

She and Adam kept running until they were out of Ghian's sight. Finally feeling safer, they stopped for a moment, massaging their aching sides.

'But . . .' panted Adam, 'she's right. We'll have to go back . . . and soon.'

Lana realized exactly what he meant. 'For Fergus,' she said between trembling breaths.

'We can't just leave him.'

Lana shook her head. 'No, we can't.' Her brother was absolutely right, and she had been absolutely wrong about Fergus – when they were in danger, he had come to help them. Now he was a prisoner of the witch, and it was their fault. She looked back up the slope behind them; for the moment the only thing coming over it was the rolling fog. 'But we can't go back there right now. We need to talk to Uncle Larry.'

'What can we tell him? Our friend, the ghost, has been captured?'

'No. If we tell him all about Ghian, he'll have to come and check out her cave for himself.'

Adam nodded slowly. 'I hope you're right.'

'I hope so too,' said Lana. 'Let's go.'

10

Somewhere on the way back to Bray, Adam and Lana left the fog behind them. Either it had thinned naturally or – supernaturally – it had preferred to remain on the cliffs. Ghian had demonstrated her command over it, and Adam wondered why she hadn't sent it in pursuit of them. Perhaps there were limits to her powers, perhaps they were just lucky – or perhaps she was right, and she knew they would be back before long.

In any case, the twins were exhausted by the time they dragged themselves into Bray. Thankfully they hadn't far to go to find Uncle Larry.

The film crew were on the promenade, just wrapping up their shoot on the Victorian seafront, lashed by swollen grey waves, all tipped with white. There was quite a wind getting up – perhaps that explained why the fog had cleared.

It was certainly the reason why Uncle Larry's

wig was flapping around so haphazardly. Angela was flapping around too, but in her brusque, trying-to-take-charge-of-everything way.

'*Right*, let's see if we can get this last little bit in one take, shall we? And – *action!*' she commanded.

'And so,' said Uncle Larry, staring mournfully into Camera One, 'this ghostly lone fisherman parades the seafront on stormy nights, watching and waiting for his drowned shipmates to find their way ashore.'

Adam and Lana summoned the strength for one last dash, waving to attract their uncle's attention. 'Uncle Larry! Uncle Larry!'

Angela looked ready to spit flame. '*Cut!*' she screeched.

'It's OK!' Dave, the cameraman, assured her. 'I think we got it!'

'You *think*? You'd better be *sure*, hadn't you?' Angela advanced on the cameraman with a menacing expression and he fumbled with the camera's controls in his haste to bring up the playback for her inspection.

Uncle Larry stuffed his rolled-up script in a pocket. 'Hello, you two. What have you been up to? You both look exhausted.'

'Uncle Larry,' said Adam breathlessly, 'you have

to come up to the stones. There's this witch, she's real. Really real. And she's got this cave and –'

'And she's practising all this black magic!' put in Lana, who was thinking the situation needed an added note of urgency. 'Honestly, Uncle Larry, you have to come and see!'

'Show him the pictures!' said Adam, digging into his sister's coat pocket for her phone.

'Hey!' said Lana.

Adam ignored her and, working the menu swiftly, he brought up the first of the photos and flashed the screen in front of Uncle Larry.

'Well, now,' said their uncle, standing back a little and looking as though he had just been presented with a jigsaw puzzle. Then he glanced apologetically at Adam. 'Um . . .'

Lana snatched her phone back. She took one look, then thrust the screen under Adam's nose. He groaned. The candles had come out as blobs of light and the rest of the picture was made up of blobs of shadow. 'See,' said Lana, 'I told you they'd be next to useless.'

'They're not next to useless,' complained Adam. 'They *are* useless. I knew I should have taken them!'

'Why? Because you believing in everything would make the pictures come out better?

Anyway, it's not my fault you didn't bring your own phone!'

'What,' said Angela, coming up behind them and making them jump, 'is all the *fuss* about?' She glared at Adam and Lana severely, like a teacher who had caught them chatting during an important test.

Uncle Larry cleared his throat. 'Hmm, well, it seems the children may have found a witch.'

Angela rolled her eyes. 'Pah! A witch. You mean they've found a local woman who "acts a bit weird" and happens to own a black cat.'

'No,' argued Lana. 'That's what I thought at first. But she's much more than that.'

'It's true!' Adam insisted. He tried to think back to some of the books he had seen on Ghian's shelves. He knew they would mean a great deal to Uncle Larry. 'She had all these really old magic books! The *Heptameron* and the *Magica de Profundis*.'

'Really?' Uncle Larry blinked, as if he'd been struck in the face with each of the weighty spellbooks. 'Those are grimoires – rare and powerful texts.'

'Oh, please!' scoffed Angela. 'They sound more like indigestion tablets.'

Uncle Larry ignored her. His gaze was alive

with fascination. 'Tell me, did you see any pentacles? They're magic symbols like five-pointed stars,' he explained, catching sight of Lana's blank expression. 'Did her cauldron have the traditional three legs? What about knives or chalices?'

Adam remembered seeing a lot of knives near the cauldron. 'There was a knife with a black handle and a plain bronze blade, no runes or symbols. It looked like a real *Athame* to me.'

'What's an *Atharmay*?' Lana had to ask.

'A witch's sacred blade,' replied Uncle Larry excitedly. 'They have replicas in the gift shop in town, but they're completely inaccurate – covered with fancy Celtic patterns. A real witch would never decorate her knives, for fear of being attacked by the Church. Of course, nobody burns witches at the stake any more, but a true witch might well keep to such traditions,' he said. 'Well, Angela, I really think this is something we should look into.'

'Hmmph! You'll be pleased to know, Larry, dear, that your last take is safely in the can. But that was more by luck than design.' Angela glowered at the twins. 'So if it's all the same to you, I think we've heard enough of this nonsense. The last thing our schedule needs right now is *children* leading us a merry dance and costing us more time and money.'

'But, Angela, you're always saying how we need to spice up our episodes a bit.' Uncle Larry swallowed, but he regarded Adam and Lana with the hint of a proud smile. 'And the children investigated it themselves. All at no extra cost.'

'Ha!' said Angela, shooting him one of her withering glares. 'And *where* did they first hear about this "witch"?'

'From a local boy,' said Lana quickly.

'The key thing is, the reported evidence is highly persuasive,' said Uncle Larry. 'The children have seen it. Adam is very knowledgeable about the supernatural, and I'm sure they wouldn't invent something like this.'

'That's right! Lana doesn't even believe in this sort of stuff,' Adam pointed out. 'She's not going to make things up.'

Uncle Larry blinked, then nodded. 'Well, there you are.' He gestured at Adam as though his words should be all the proof Angela needed. Then, because Angela's expression was still like a closed door, he added a meek appeal: 'And even if the woman turns out to be just an interesting local character, I think a short interview might add a splash of colour and —'

'Oh, stop right there. People are not going to

switch on to watch some batty old crone prattling about magic.'

'Actually, she's kind of young,' Adam said.

'In a strange sort of way,' added Lana. 'She's got a young face but she says she's older than she looks.'

'Old, young. Makes no difference. Batty crones *aren't* ratings winners.'

'She's not just some lady,' insisted Adam angrily. 'She's a witch!'

'You'd only need to take one look at her cave to see that,' said Lana, appealing to Angela earnestly. 'One look!'

Uncle Larry swallowed and steeled himself to look Angela in the eye. 'Now, Angela, why don't you listen to them. The show needs more material – you're always saying that yourself. We can't afford to pass this up.' His firmness was almost convincing, but unfortunately his stomach chose just that moment to growl loudly. 'We have to go up to the stones anyway for tonight's shoot,' he said hopefully, speaking loudly to cover more gurgles and growls.

'Yes,' said Angela at length, and behind her icy gaze Adam and Lana could see she was thinking it over. 'Very well. We can take a look after dinner. It's been a long, tiring day, and if we must have another all-night vigil then I want a hot meal inside me first. And you, Larry, should do the same. We don't want your tummy-rumbles coming through during a take.'

Uncle Larry smiled weakly.

'But we need to go now,' Adam pleaded.

'Why? This cave won't be going anywhere, will it? No,' said Angela flatly, 'we'll check it out after dinner when we're in the vicinity anyway. And that is my *final* word.' And with that she stalked off to make sure the crew were completing the packing-up operation to her satisfaction.

Adam and Lana sagged.

Uncle Larry must have heard their sighs because he laid his hands on their shoulders in sympathy. 'Don't you worry, now. We'll check out your cave, all right. And if she's any kind of self-respecting witch, she'll wait until midnight before getting up to any really exciting magic. It is the witching hour, remember.'

He grinned and looked excited at the prospect of the evening ahead.

Adam and Lana did their best to return his smile. It was small consolation for poor Fergus, but they just had to take what they could get.

11

Dinner seemed to go on forever. Time seemed to take pleasure in being stubborn. The faster Adam and Lana wanted it to go, the more time dragged its heels. They both skipped dessert – this time voluntarily – but Angela insisted on enquiring about cheese and biscuits and rounding off her dinner with coffee.

Thankfully, Mrs Flanaghan didn't provide these, so finally Adam and Lana could excuse themselves and rush upstairs to fetch their coats – and a couple of torches. But then there was more waiting while the crew collected their own gear. Even Uncle Larry joined them waiting. Eager and full of energy, he paced the floor and made impatient little huffs every time he examined his watch.

It wasn't until well after eight that they set off.

'It's been ages,' groaned Adam as they trudged up the hill. He and his sister were in the lead, doing what they could to set a brisk pace.

'I know,' sympathized Lana. 'But perhaps Uncle Larry's right. If Ghian is going to do anything to poor Fergus, she might hold off until midnight.'

'Maybe,' agreed Adam, but they were both aware that Ghian had done plenty of witching earlier, regardless of the hour. 'If she does, that would give us loads of time.' He checked his watch (for the tenth time since they had left the guest house) and stole a glance back at the crew, hauling their equipment and casually chatting as they ambled along. 'But at this rate, it could take hours to get there.'

Only Uncle Larry was forging ahead of the pack, an eager spring in his long stride. He looked like a man on a mission and for once seemed entirely unconcerned about what the wind might be doing to his wig.

'But when we do get there, we'll have a small army with us,' smiled Lana helpfully.

Adam had to give in to a laugh at that. 'True. Ghian won't know what's hit her.'

'Especially Angela. She'd scare anyone – even a witch.'

Lana nudged her brother and nodded towards

Steve, who was bringing up the rear, doing a poor job of concealing a shoebox with the bulky sleeve of his parka. 'Do you think we should warn Uncle Larry that Angela's planning to use the Banshee?'

'No,' Adam decided. 'Once she's seen Ghian and Fergus, she won't be needing that thing.'

'All righty,' said Angela, when they were in sight of the stones, 'you lot get set up. Larry and I will investigate this "witch's lair". We *won't* be long,' she added with special emphasis and a look intended chiefly for Adam and Lana.

Uncle Larry gave the children an encouraging wink and tapped his nose. 'We might be longer than she thinks if your story's as good as it sounds.'

The twins led Angela and their uncle past the stones to the stacked rock formation. Angela peered unenthusiastically down into the cleft in the rocks, but Uncle Larry flicked his torch on and descended straight away.

The route was fairly obvious, despite the dark. Uncle Larry had to duck a little on the staircase, but he wore an eager grin, as excited as any young boy might be at finding a cave. He opened his mouth to say something, but Lana cut him off with a finger to her lips.

'She might hear us,' she whispered.

'Oh,' said Angela out loud, then – at the sound of her echoing voice – thought better of it and whispered, 'What *nonsense*.'

Uncle Larry sped down the passage. Adam and Lana stayed close to him and left Angela to bring up the rear. Just a few more steps . . .

'Oh dear,' said their uncle as they arrived at the foot of the stairs. His shoulders slumped.

Adam and Lana came round on either side of him.

Adam's face fell. So did Lana's. They frowned and gaped at each other.

'But . . .' blurted Adam.

'That's not . . .' began his sister.

'It's not anything,' observed Angela scathingly. She had come to a halt on the step above, which gave her an ample view over Uncle Larry's head. The cavern was empty, except for a rough stone table, the remains of an old camp fire and a few scattered bits of junk littering the ground. 'It's just a *cave*. With a spot of set-dressing it might look like something, but right now it's just a yawning hole in the ground. So forgive me if I out-yawn it. Come along, Larry, we've got real work to do.'

'Angela,' suggested Uncle Larry weakly, 'don't you think we should get some shots of –'

'Of what?'

Adam and Lana could only carry on staring as the argument echoed round them.

'Of the cave. I mean, it must be directly under the stones.' Uncle Larry shone his torch up at the roof, wheeling the beam about erratically like a rather drunken searchlight. 'That may be of great significance. This cave might be quite a find on its own. Who knows what ancient rituals may have taken place here.'

'Exactly!' barked Angela. 'Who knows? And who will care?'

Uncle Larry's beam swung disappointedly down to find Angela, and her eyes blazed in the torchlight. 'Possibly, maybe,' she said, 'if we're not all too worn out by then, we might get a panning shot around the cavern. Heaven knows, this episode will need plenty of *padding*. But only after we're done with the shoot at the stones and every scripted scene is in the can. Now, come along! Time is money!'

She stomped off up the steps.

Uncle Larry let out a weighty sigh, like he was deflating. 'Well, I can't argue with that.' He patted Adam and Lana on the shoulders. 'Come along, children.'

'But, Uncle Larry –'

'It's all changed,' declared Adam. 'There was more here. Much more.'

'It's true,' said Lana desperately. 'There was a cauldron, benches and potions, and a tapestry. A great long tapestry – and hundreds of candles!'

'Well,' suggested their uncle, 'perhaps someone came and cleared it all away. Maybe the local children were having a game with you. Or, if you two had something to do with it, I suppose I should thank you for trying. I know you want the show to succeed. But you know I don't care for fakery and theatrics. Now, let's go and search for some real ghosts, eh?'

Looking as though the entire cavern roof had fallen on him, he headed off up the staircase.

Adam and Lana stayed put. Neither of them knew what to say. They swept their torch beams over the cavern, both feeling positively gloomy.

Lana sighed. 'We know she can cast illusions,' she said. 'She cast that illusion of herself before.'

'True,' agreed Adam, surveying the cavern again. He frowned, as though trying to see through the magic. If, indeed, there had ever been anything magical here.

But now he was beginning to think like his sister – unwilling to believe the evidence of what he had seen with his own eyes. Adam felt like switching his torch off and giving up.

But just as he pushed his thumb against the switch, something happened.

Lana gasped.

A shimmer passed like ripples over the cavern, from the centre outwards – as though someone had dropped a stone into a reflection in a pool. As the ripples spread, everything under their magical surface was transformed, and the cavern changed back to just the way they had found it earlier. The benches, the cauldron, the potions, the tapestry, the loom, they were all there. Watched over by hundreds of flickering candles.

'I knew it!' said Adam, and he clenched his fist. 'Let's get Uncle Larry!'

He turned to shout up the staircase.

'Oh, thank goodness!' said a familiar voice. 'Hey, you two! It's me, Fergus.'

Adam and Lana swung round, sweeping this way and that with their torches. There was no sign of the little ghost. 'Fergus! Where are you? Come on out!' Lana called.

'I'm not hiding,' the boy hissed. Adam strained to pinpoint the direction of his voice. 'I'm over here!'

Lana aimed her torch. 'Somewhere over there. By the loom,' she said.

Lana stepped down off the stairs and lightly crossed the cave. Adam followed, glancing all around in case Ghian decided to show up.

'Here! Over here!' repeated Fergus. 'Come on, you're getting warmer. Red hot!'

Adam and Lana sent their torch beams roaming all over the cavern, wondering if Fergus was hiding in the wall again. But there was not even the hint of a nose poking out. It was only when he said, 'Hello! Right in front of you!' that Lana suddenly thought to shine her torch at the tapestry.

And there was Fergus, looking back out at them. Woven into the fabric like all the other illustrations.

12

Above ground, Angela was not best pleased.

For one thing, the weather was proving uncooperative. An eerie mist was creeping in, helping to generate a suitably ghoulish atmosphere, but there was none of the rain and wind that they had endured the night before. Which meant they wouldn't be able to cut in any of last night's footage. They would have to re-shoot everything from scratch.

And another thing, the crew were as disorganized as usual, full of questions about where they should set up and what they were supposed to be doing. And for a third, Uncle Larry was being his usual crazy self, insisting that they maintain at least a six-hour vigil to give any potential ghosts sufficient time to make an appearance. Angela was a natural-born leader, she always believed, but she had little patience with the living let alone the dead. It seemed as if the Shrieking Stones were the only things behaving in accordance with her wishes – all they had to do was stand around in a circle.

And now, just as their preparations were finishing, she discovered that something else had gone wrong. 'Larry!' she called. '*Where* are those children?'

'Hmm?' Uncle Larry peered round like a man who had misplaced his glasses. He stood up straight when the truth hit home. 'Children? Well, I suppose they must still be down in the cave. Probably disappointed their witch's lair won't be making it into the show.'

'And neither will *they* if they don't get a move on.'

Uncle Larry couldn't see the angry gleam in her eye from where he stood, but he heard the tone of her voice. 'I'll, um, just go and check on them, shall I?' He coughed nervously.

'You will do no such thing,' Angela fumed, drawing herself up. 'I'm not having them hold us up any longer. If we must stand here for six hours waiting for a ghost to drop in, then I say that six hours starts right now.' There were gratifying murmurs of approval from some of the crew. 'If the children don't show up, we go ahead without them.'

Angela then glimpsed Steve, who was loitering by one of the larger stones that guarded the outer edge of the circle and trying to attract her attention with a wave. He grinned oafishly and gave her a thumbs-up sign.

Angela understood, and smiled to herself. That was something else going according to plan at least. If, as she expected, no ghosts had appeared by the end of the shoot, she would give the signal to unleash the Banshee – whether Larry liked it or not.

Down in the cave, Adam and Lana stared breathlessly and shone their torches at the tapestry for a closer look.

As amazing as their first encounter with Fergus had been, it was even more incredible to see him rendered in such intricate detail with such fine stitchwork. His tiny form was shown in colour, rather than his normal ghostly white, and despite being embroidered he managed to blink at them and throw up his arm in front of his face.

'Hey, do you mind! The light's right in my eyes!'

Adam and Lana moved their torches aside.

'It's incredible,' said Lana. 'How did she –'

'How do you think? With that loom of hers.'

Fergus waved his stitchwork arms. 'Take a look. That's the bottle she had me in, over there on the loom.' Lana looked, and sure enough there was the blue bottle, upturned and mounted on a kind of spindle at one end of the loom. Faintly glowing threads stretched from the loom into the neck of the bottle. 'Whatever fabric us spirits are made of, she weaves into her stupid tapestry.'

'Why didn't you tell us?' said Adam.

'I only just found out. The hard way. And believe me, it was no joke.'

'Bet she had you in stitches!' wisecracked Adam, unable to resist.

Fergus's embroidered features wove themselves into a frown. 'Hey, this is no laughing matter. Once that loom gets hold of you, that's it. Those threads you see attached to it – they sink into you like roots, and start pulling you apart, like you're just made up of a whole lot of strings. Then before you know it, the loom goes to work knitting you into not a very pretty picture! I'm trapped in here now and you're mocking me.'

'Sorry,' said Lana. 'Hold on while we think of a way to get you out of there.'

'Well, think quickly. She'll be back any minute.'

Lana glanced nervously around. There was no

sign of Ghian, but the candlelit cavern was full of shadowy nooks and crannies where the witch could be hiding. She could even be watching them at that very moment . . . Lana shuddered.

'Hurry up, Adam,' she whispered.

Her brother was searching along the length of the tapestry, picking out all the illustrated figures they had seen before. 'So, are all these people, these pictures, really ghosts she's captured and woven into this thing?'

'That'd be my guess. I remember feeling other ghosts being dragged away out of the stones while I was trapped in them myself. But I never knew what became of them until now. It's not like I can go for a stroll along the tapestry and ask someone,' said Fergus glumly. 'I can move my arms and my handsome features, but that's about it. I'm stuck in place.'

'That's dreadful,' Lana sympathized. But she wondered what on earth they could do to rescue him. From her brother's expression, she could tell he was thinking the same.

'And I don't think that's the worst of it,' Fergus carried on. 'The others aren't able to move or talk at all. I reckon if I stay woven into this for too long, I'll become just another part of the tapestry like that lot.'

'And you don't fancy being a man of the cloth?' said Adam.

'Stop that. I'm not in much of a mood for jokes.'

In answer to Fergus's scowl, Adam gave a look of apology. 'Well, why is Ghian doing it? And if she can draw ghosts directly out of the stones, why did she collect you in a bottle? It's just crazy.'

'Maybe not,' said Lana, trying to think things through logically. 'Perhaps it's just easier for her to capture the ghosts *before* they get caught in the stones, if she can.'

Adam gave his sister a considered nod, as though he felt she might be on to something. Although he was fairly sure that couldn't be the whole story. 'What do you think, Fergus?'

The miniature Fergus gave a shrug. 'I don't know. I'm more inclined to believe your theory – that she's just crazy. It's anybody's guess.'

'The polite thing to do would be to just ask,' said Ghian. 'And it's really not nice to go calling people crazy.'

Adam and Lana whirled round, finding themselves facing the witch – who looked delighted to see them. 'You're welcome back to my humble home. But I trust you'll do me the kindness of staying for longer this time.'

Ghian reached up and yanked a thorny twig from her tangled hair, and tossed it to the ground in front of them. She chanted:

'A sprig of thicket
Is just the ticket
To keep these monsters caged!'

Amid a flash and a puff of smoke, the twig sprouted rapidly, branches forking in all directions like thorny lightning, forming into a cage around them. Adam and Lana huddled close together, retreating from Ghian's evil cackles as well as the thorns on the still-growing bars of their prison.

13

Adam's first impulse was to take hold of the bars and shake them. The cage was only a tangled mesh of flimsy branches, but since every bit of those twigs was covered with vicious-looking thorns he decided to keep his hands at his side. At their feet, the branches disappeared into the ground, apparently taking root.

Adam and Lana were stuck.

Ghian stalked around the outside of their bramble prison, looking terribly pleased with her two fresh captives. Adam had lowered his torch, but Lana kept hers on the witch.

A thought seemed to cross Ghian's mind and her expression darkened instantly. 'So,' she sighed, 'now you know the secret of my tapestry. How dull. Not my tapestry, of course – that's really a beautiful piece of work, even though I say so myself. No, what's dull is that you know the secret. People knowing tends to take the shine off a secret, don't you think? The fewer the better, I say. So, what do you say, we just keep this one between ourselves?'

Ghian's eyes glinted menacingly as she drew nearer, peering in at them through the thorny bars.

'What do you want with them?' Lana demanded defiantly, shining her torch right in the witch's face.

'Excuse me?'

'All the ghosts,' said Adam. 'Why are you weaving them into your tapestry?'

Ghian looked at him disdainfully, and Adam felt the need to add, 'You said the polite thing was to ask.'

'Oh yes. But that doesn't guarantee you any answers, dear. No, no, there are no guarantees in life. Or even afterwards. Isn't that right, boy?' She glowered at the tapestry, addressing Fergus. 'Still,' she said, 'the thing about life – or indeed death – is to make the most of it. Which is what I intend to do very shortly.'

Without warning, Ghian's hands lashed out, faster than the twins' eyes could follow, and snatched their torches from them, aiming the beams into their own eyes. Confined by their thorny cell, Adam and Lana couldn't even throw up their arms to shield themselves from the glare.

'But since you two are going to be taking part,' crowed Ghian, 'I suppose you deserve to know a little. It's only polite.' She tossed the torches behind her and they hit the cavern floor with a double thud and clatter. The beams died instantly, abandoning the cave to shadows and candlelight.

'Ghosts,' said Ghian, 'ghosts are powerful things. There's much more energy in a single ghost than in these modern torches. Oh yes, a torch will last a few hours – but a ghost, a ghost might last forever.'

'Fergus did say he was made of energy,' remarked Adam.

'So you're after their power?' said Lana. She could understand that, at least. She and her brother had seen enough movies to know that power was the one thing villains wanted above everything else. 'But what for? And why Fergus especially? Did he really get all your witch friends caught and burned? Or did you make that up?'

'Oh, I may have exaggerated a little,' agreed Ghian casually, 'but it was all true in the essentials.'

'You're lying,' accused Adam.

'Bah! The boy is a menace, with his pranks

and jokes. Especially as a ghost. All his poltergeistly tricks attracting the wrong attention, bringing people straight to our doors.'

'I was only playing,' declared Fergus from the tapestry. 'It's not my fault if you witches were up to no good when they came knocking.'

'Shut your mouth, boy – before Auntie Ghian sews it up!' Ghian tossed back her head and laughed, excessively amused with herself. She glared at the twins but pointed airily in Fergus's direction. 'So, as I was saying, he used to be trouble. But he's so much more than that. He's powerful. More powerful than he knows. See, children can make the most powerful ghosts. They've all their lives ahead of them, you see. Years and years of energy they never have the opportunity to use up when they're alive.' Ghian tenderly ran a hand across the tapestry, as if she could feel the power in the cloth. Her fingernails lingered over the little woven Fergus, as though she were considering scratching his tiny stitchwork eyes out.

Adam nudged his sister and quietly whispered, 'We should do something.'

Lana made a face and shrugged. 'Like what?' she mouthed.

Ghian drew herself up, gesturing proudly at the length of the tapestry. 'And you can see how many ghosts I've collected. All worked into the tapestry by the power of my loom. They were drawn here by the stones, like moths to a great flame in the heart of the land. A lot of them were my sisters – fellow witches – and they were powerful because of their magic, of course. And they are all commemorated here, their lives shown in threads of colour.' More dismissively, she added, 'While a lot of ordinary, common spirits – ghosts of nobodies, you might say – have gone to make up the plain background.' Then her eyes were on fire again. 'But the boy, he was special, one of the most powerful of the lot.' She gave a twisted smile that, in the candlelight, seemed to twitch and writhe like a snake. 'Oh, he was powerful enough to escape from me once. And you, my dears, went and released him from the stones. So . . .' She clapped her hands happily and sighed, 'I owe you my gratitude. Thank you both.'

'Huh,' grouched Adam. 'Next time, do it yourself.'

Ghian froze, and shot Adam a look that was like a blast of icy wind. And suddenly, the penny dropped.

'You couldn't, could you?' said Adam. 'That's why Fergus was trapped in the stones for so long! You couldn't release him yourself. You had to wait for someone to come along and touch the stones for you.'

'But why?' asked Lana, confused.

'It's like Fergus told us – only the touch of a mortal could release him.'

'But that would mean –'

'She's a ghost!' Fergus piped up from his clothbound prison. 'Like me!'

'The ghost of a witch,' nodded Adam. 'That's how she grabbed our torches just now without getting scratched.'

'But that's impossible,' said Lana. 'What's keeping her from getting sucked into the stones?'

'Us ghosts!' said Fergus angrily. 'She's got all of us sewn up in her precious tapestry. All our energy. More than enough to resist the pull of the stones, right?'

'Oh, you're right, for all the good it will do you. I *am* a ghost.' Ghian flashed a nasty grin. 'For the present, at least.'

'That's why you take everything so personally,' said Adam. 'Everything that happened to those witches through the ages. That happened to you too.'

'What did they do?' wondered Lana uneasily. 'Did they drown you? Or burn you at the stake?'

'Does it matter? Does it make a difference?'

Ghian's icy gaze turned to flame. 'As of tonight, all that is of no account.'

Ghian crossed to her loom and seized the bottle that had once contained poor Fergus. Caressing the blue glass, she carefully lifted it from the spindle, cupping her hand to prevent the contents from spilling out. Turning it the right way up, the witch gently shook the bottle, and it made the same sinister rattle as it had done before. Finally, fixing the children with a calculating look, she announced, 'Yes, I should think this will do. You two are very close. You won't mind a tight squeeze.'

'What are you talking about?' demanded Adam, growing angry as well as scared.

Ghian tutted and touched a finger to her lips. 'Shush, patience. First things first.'

Plucking at the glowing threads that ran from the bottle to the loom as if she was playing a musical instrument, Ghian teased them loose. Freed from the bottle, they hung slack for a moment. Then, as Adam and Lana watched, the enchanted threads seemed to take on a life of their own, twitching uncertainly and rising into the air like a mass of very thin serpents at the command of a snake charmer. Ghian raised her arms and – obedient to their mistress – the threads shot up towards the roof of the cave, where they hung like the fan-shaped silvery strings of a great harp, stretching up from the loom to disappear into the rocky shadows above.

'What's that for?' asked Lana, as defiant – and just as scared – as her brother.

'Oh, don't worry. It's not for you, child. Not yet, anyway. Every new subject in my tapestry needs appropriate background material.'

'They're the threads Fergus was telling us about,' remarked Adam. 'The ones that drew him out of the bottle. It's like Uncle Larry said, this cave is directly under the Shrieking Stones. She's setting her threads to reach right up into them.'

'Drawing the ghosts out directly,' Lana said, following the threads with her eyes and imagining them like roots, plunging upward into the earth to feed. She looked at Ghian. 'But isn't that going to take a lot of energy? If the stones are like a big magnet, pulling ghosts in, then your loom is going to have to fight that to drag the ghosts out, surely?'

'Ah,' Ghian winked, 'you're a bright young miss. You understand how it all works. Of course, every girl should know the art of embroidery.' She laughed. 'You see, common ghosts can be enticed easily enough from the stones. My loom has more than enough magic to lure them. Only the special ones – the spirits of my witch sisters or those of children – are too powerful, too resistant. And, it goes without saying, in the case of children, downright stubborn.'

'Which is why you captured Fergus in a bottle the first time,' concluded Lana. Filled with chippings taken from the stones and whatever spells Ghian had cast upon it, the bottle would act like a handheld vacuum cleaner, hoovering up a ghost like Fergus before he could be sucked into the stones.

'Precisely.' Ghian gave a sour smile, like she had swallowed half a lemon. 'But then the idiot boy escaped and got himself stuck in the stones. And so it was an age – more than a century – before you two came along and released the lad to me.'

'But you've got Fergus in the tapestry now. So why do you need more "ordinary" ghosts for your background?' asked Adam, with a nasty suspicion that he wasn't going to like the answer.

'It doesn't matter why! There aren't any ghosts left up there, you stupid witch!' hollered Fergus. Adam and Lana supposed he had nothing left to fear from Ghian now, as he was trapped in the fabric already. 'I was the last one. You've drained those stones dry of spirits. They're all here in this length of old rag with me.'

'Powerful the boy may be, but he's not very bright.' Ghian gestured at the high roof. 'The weather, magic, ghosts – they are all different forms of the same energies, and they are all at my command. All I need do is call down a lightning bolt or two and there'll be a fresh supply of ghosts in the stones. Quick as a flash.'

'Uncle Larry and the crew!' realized Lana, horrified.

The evil cunning of Ghian's plan took Adam's breath away. He thought of the crew filming above their heads, unaware of what was going on beneath them. Even Angela didn't deserve to be made into a ghost and woven into a tapestry.

'They'll be ideal material, I should think,' Ghian mused. 'And another reason I should thank you. You thought you were so clever, bringing all those other people along with you, but you've only brought them right where I want them!'

'You can't!' Lana shouted at Ghian. 'You can't do that!'

'Oh, don't fret, child.' Ghian's voice had turned soothing, but it was cold comfort indeed. 'You'll be reunited with them soon enough. They'll make a splendid background for the final additions to my tapestry.' She came strolling over, stroking the blue glass bottle like it was a treasured pet. 'Do you know what I'm missing? What I need to complete my life's work?'

She drew very near the thorny cage and leaned in to smile softly at them.

'No! And we don't care!' shouted Adam, although it was a lie.

'Just two more ghosts!' declared Ghian cheerfully. 'All I need to complete my journey! Two special, powerful ghosts.'

Adam swallowed, his throat dry, as he looked at his sister. It was painfully clear what Ghian meant: two more child ghosts. Adam had been amazed by Fergus's powers, but those same supernatural abilities were suddenly a lot less cool now that he was threatened with the prospect of becoming a ghost himself.

The witch's eyes sparkled dangerously. She spread her arms wide and tipped her head back as though to throw her voice at the heavens:

'*I call upon the thunder*
To tear the skies asunder
And slay with deadly bolts!'

Ghian let out a satisfied sigh. 'There,' she said, 'that ought to do it.'

And as if in agreement, from somewhere far above came the unmistakable rumble of a distant storm.

14

Up at the Shrieking Stones, the weather was deteriorating rapidly. Lightning flashed far out over the sea and the accompanying thunder seemed to get closer by the minute. A rising wind had blown in heavy rainclouds almost out of nowhere, and now the heavens opened.

As well as wet, the weather was making Uncle Larry jittery and nervous. Between takes, he paced up and down and struck his head with the rolled-up script, as though drumming the words into his skull. The rest of the crew were waterlogged and miserable.

But for Angela, safely wrapped in her expensive state-of-the-art waterproofs, the rain was excellent news. It was like a re-run of the night before, only without the kids – which suited her fine. If the storm really picked up, they would even be able to match in some of the previous night's footage after all.

'This is more like it,' she declared to everyone in general.

As if in response, the wind blew even harder, wailing through the stones like a tormented spirit.

Below, in the cavern, the boom of thunder was a reminder to Adam and Lana that they were not the only ones in danger.

'Twins!' Ghian declared. 'You can't get a much more powerful combination than that. A conjunction of souls! Yes, more than sufficient to complete my tapestry – and complete me. I have such a lot to thank you for. Tonight, thanks to you, I will complete my journey from ghost to mortal.'

'That's what all this is about?' said Lana. 'You're using all the energy of those other ghosts to bring yourself back to life?'

'Yeah, and your so-called sisters – your fellow witches too. I'll bet they're happy about that,' said Adam.

'Oh, a few would object. The selfish, short-sighted ones. But most would admit to a grudging admiration, I'm sure. Besides,' Ghian cupped a hand to her ear, 'I don't hear any complaints. Anyway, I was the one who had the idea. I was the one who created the magical loom. I was the one who slaved for centuries over this work of art. I do so tire of being a ghost. Now, how would you prefer to die?'

'Not at all, thanks,' answered Lana.

'Oh, but it's much better if you choose,' Ghian recommended. 'You'll go peacefully, prepared. As ghosts, you'll be much more cooperative – much less stubborn.'

'You leave them alone!' Fergus warned the witch sternly.

'Oh, do be quiet!' Ghian snapped. Then she smiled at Adam and Lana, but the madness in her eyes was plain to see, even by candlelight. 'See, you wouldn't want to end up like the boy, now would you? Never mind, you discuss it among yourselves.' She danced off towards her cauldron, set the blue bottle down and began picking through some of the equipment laid out on the bench-top. 'And if you find you can't make up your minds, I've plenty of sharp instruments that will do the job very beautifully.'

By way of example, she held up the bronze dagger with the black handle, the *Athame*. 'What do you think of this one?' She laid it down in favour of a longer knife with a cruel, serrated blade. 'Or this?'

An especially loud thunderclap seemed to applaud her choice.

Lana stared at her brother. She looked pale and too frightened to speak. Adam squeezed her hand to reassure her. He didn't know how, but he wanted to hold on to the idea that they were going to be OK. And he needed his sister to hold on to that thought too.

Then he searched her eyes and saw a glimmer a lot like hope. Adam recognized that his sister had an idea and nearly smiled – until he remembered Ghian might be watching. Instead he gave her a simple, short nod. Whatever she tried, he would back her up.

From her pocket, Lana produced her mobile phone. 'Well,' she announced loudly, 'I'm not standing around here waiting for you to kill us! I'm going to call for help. And warn Uncle Larry and everybody up there.'

Adam glimpsed the signal bar on the phone's screen. Just as he suspected, there was no signal at all so far underground. But the witch wouldn't know that – would she? Lana keyed in some numbers and held the phone to her ear.

The effect was more dramatic than even Lana

expected. Ghian whirled round, wild-eyed, and ran at their cage. 'Give me that!' she screamed. 'You people think you can harness magicks with your devices and contraptions. Well, you can't! And you can't call your friends! You're here now and you're mine!'

Once again, her hand lashed out, shooting through the thorny bars. But Lana was ready for her this time. The thorny bars of the cage prevented her snatching her hand away, but she kept a firm grip on the phone and Ghian couldn't prise it away from her.

'No way!' Lana said, sticking her tongue out. 'If you want this, you'll have to come in and get it!'

'Impudent, spiteful girl! Well, if that's the way you wish to play, I'll cut that tongue of yours out and we'll have no more of your backchat! You won't be needing it where you're going!'

Raising her knife high, Ghian hacked at the mesh of branches that imprisoned the twins, as if she was cutting her way through a thick jungle. With just a few swipes of the blade, she was through and staring furiously down at them as the cage fell apart, the thorny branches disintegrating into so much sawdust and powder.

Whatever his sister had planned next, this was

Adam's moment. He had to buy her some time. Luckily, Fergus had given him tips on just how to do that.

Adam ducked and bolted to the right. Ghian made a grab for him, but he slipped just past her reach and was away. Darting for the nearest shelves, he leaped up and swept a hand along the rows of bottles and jars. They tumbled to the ground and shattered, scattering glass and echoes all around.

Ghian seethed and spat. Another crash of thunder from above, the loudest yet, seemed to echo her fury. She shoved Lana aside, chasing after Adam, with her knife in hand and a murderous look in her eye.

'Go, Adam!' whooped Fergus.

While her brother ran riot around the cavern, smashing everything in sight and generally creating havoc, Lana rushed to the bench-top beside the cauldron and snatched up Ghian's magical blue bottle as well as another of the witch's knives. It was shorter, with a much less threatening blade, but it would be enough for her needs.

Lana glanced at Ghian: she was scarily close, but her attention was fixed on Adam. The witch had spread her arms wide and was closing in on her prey, ready to cut him off whichever way he went. Adam tried a feint, dodging left, then immediately switching to the right. It caught Ghian momentarily off-balance, but she lunged after him with the knife. She was quick, and missed Adam only by millimetres.

Running across the floor, he managed to bring more jars and chalices crashing down from the shelves. The cavern was filled with the din of breaking glass, the clatter of falling metal, Ghian's enraged yells and the earth-shattering clamour of the storm.

Lana couldn't afford to worry about her brother. She ran to the loom.

Lana knew nothing of magic. Although she had to believe in it now, she supposed, she was far from understanding it. But she thought she understood how the loom worked. Like a computer it had an input and an output. Ghosts were fed in at one end through the glowing, enchanted threads, the loom worked its magic, and cloth emerged from the other. Ghian had already admitted that the cloth – her tapestry of ghosts – was the source of her power. And, like when she had snagged her favourite jumper on a splinter, Lana knew that cloth could easily unravel . . .

Biting her lip and hoping she was right, she slashed at the tapestry with her knife.

'Hey! Watch what you're doing with that thing!' cried Fergus.

'Sorry,' replied Lana, cutting at the material again, careful to avoid Fergus's woven body. Soon, the tapestry was completely severed from the loom. The cloth drooped, its loose, frayed ends brushing the floor.

Without wasting another moment, Lana hurled Ghian's precious bottle – the bottle the witch had meant to catch *them* in – to the ground with a smash. Sure enough, among the bits of blue glass, right under the loose ends of the tapestry, lay several small chippings taken from the Shrieking Stones. Steadily, the fibres of the tapestry began to respond. Answering the pull of the miniature stones, the tapestry began to unravel.

'*What have you done?!*' screamed Ghian, in a voice louder than the thunder. She had stopped in her tracks, her eyes bulging insanely at Lana's destructive efforts.

It was just as well: behind her, Adam was cornered, his back pressed against the far wall. He had nowhere else to run.

'If a few little stones can lure ghosts into a bottle,' shouted Lana, 'then they can certainly pull them out of your stupid tapestry!'

Ghian watched, horrified, as her life's work

unravelled. The tattered edge of the tapestry was dissolving into smoky wisps that sailed upward, spreading out like smears of white paint upon the air. Most took on the vague outline of figures, with blurry hands and smudged faces. Others were more detailed figures with distinct features – like Fergus had been, except try as she might, Lana couldn't pick out the boy in the swirl of spirits. But she knew he had to be in there somewhere. The tapestry was returning to its original form: ghosts. Countless ghosts.

At the other end of the loom, the fan-like spread of magical, glowing threads that had stretched up to the roof, waiting to draw the ghosts of the crew from the Shrieking Stones, dropped to the ground. For a moment, they lay slack, but then they seemed to come to life again, curling about as if trying to catch an elusive scent. The threads had sensed the ghosts being released in the cave, and now they were hunting for them.

But as the tapestry continued to unravel, faster and faster, the escaping ghosts seemed to get caught in a whirlpool, like phantasmal paint sucked up into an upside-down plughole. Round and round they churned, like a ghostly tornado, as the pull of the stones drew them up towards the roof of the cave. Some opened their shadowy mouths and cried out, their voices merging like a howling wind.

Ghian's screams joined the chorus. '*Noooooooooo!*'

'Hey! Way to go, Lana!' Adam cheered.

He shouldn't have done. Enraged, Ghian rounded on him. Lifting the jagged knife, she brought the blade swiftly down.

'*Adam!*' Lana's heart stopped cold.

Out of the swirl of ghosts overhead, something swooped in at the witch. It seemed to catch hold of her cloak and pull her backwards. Adam felt a rush of wind as the knife slashed past his nose.

Cursing, Ghian struggled to keep her footing as she was dragged across the cavern, away from Adam. Fergus's laughter rebounded around the walls. 'A ghost! That's all the loom wants! Those threads are trying to get hold of a ghost!'

Suddenly Fergus's voice was cut short. As he pulled Ghian towards the loom, he strayed too close to the whirlpool of ghosts being sucked up into the stones. The boy was whipped away as though by a violent wind.

'Fergus!' Adam cried out, and he and Lana watched helplessly as their friend disappeared into the tornado of fellow phantoms.

Ghian shrieked like a maniac and turned to face Lana, raising her blade high.

Which was when one of the flailing threads from the loom lashed out like a whip and coiled around her wrist.

For a moment the witch stared at the glowing thread, puzzled. She tried to wrench her arm free, but a second thread caught her other hand. She tried to pull away again, but it was too late – more and more threads latched on to her, like evil white vines. Robbed of its connection to the tapestry, the magical loom was trying to weave a new picture. And without the power of her tapestry to protect her, Ghian was now just like any other ghost – ideal raw material.

'*Aaaaaaaaagh!*' Ghian screamed shrilly and wildly, thrashing about violently as the fatal threads wove their way around her and even *into* her, as her loom went into action. Colours started draining from her face and clothes, as she became watery and faint, just like Fergus had been.

Adam and Lana stared as Ghian came unravelled like an old pullover teased apart by invisible claws. She kicked and screamed and fought as her own ghostly form was unwound and drawn into her precious loom. The machine went dutifully to work, weaving the fresh fibres as quickly as Ghian's spiders had spun their webs of fog.

Within the loom's frame, a new pattern was taking shape before Adam and Lana's eyes. And in the centre, just coming into being, thread by thread, was a small image of Ghian. The attention to detail, in her clothing and her features, was incredible. Her miniature woven face was contorted and she was still screaming, although whether in agony or rage, it was hard to tell. A fresh length of cloth began emerging from the loom, starting to decorate the cavern with a new tapestry.

Neither of the twins felt like waiting around to see it finished.

'Come on,' Adam beckoned to his sister. 'Let's get out of here.'

'Yes,' said Lana, 'let's.'

As the twins ran for the steps, they looked for one last time at the swirling stream of ghosts disappearing into the roof. Somewhere among them was poor Fergus, drawn into the spinning current, but they couldn't make him out and they couldn't do anything for him from down here. Together with his fellow spirits he was being funnelled up into the earth above.

There was no fighting the stones.

Adam and Lana burst out of the cavern, dashed

through the cleft and ran flat out towards the lights of the film crew.

The skies were overcast and a thick blanket of fog still hugged the ground. But there was no thunder or lightning and the winds were beginning to ease, while the rain felt almost like a refreshing shower after their imprisonment below ground. The main thing was they knew the weather was no longer the work of a witch but just the usual Irish climate.

They could make out the figures of the crew working at the stones: Uncle Larry, Angela – and Steve, outside the circle, standing by with his Banshee.

Well, at least they could spare them any need for that.

They shouted as they ran. 'Uncle Larry! The stones! Touch the stones!'

Angela stiffened immediately and rounded on them. '*What* is the meaning of –?'

'Trust us!' yelled Lana. 'Touch the stones!'

'Everyone!' urged Adam. 'Touch them! Anywhere! Everywhere!'

Uncle Larry was as bemused as Angela, but he leaped straight into action, racing to the nearest of the great stones and laying a hand on its surface.

Nothing happened.

'Hang on!' Adam shouted. 'It takes a minute to start!'

Panting, the twins ran into the great circle – just as the first of the ghosts escaped like a silvery breath from the top of the stone Uncle Larry was touching. There was something almost angelic about the way it rose gracefully into the air.

The figure spread its arms like dove's wings and flapped about, enjoying its first taste of fresh air, perhaps for centuries. Its face was indistinct and blurry, and it was impossible to say whether this ghost had been a man or a woman, an ordinary mortal or one of Ghian's witch sisters, but one thing Adam and Lana could see for sure: it was smiling.

'Everybody! Come on!' urged Adam again.

And he and his sister joined in with Uncle Larry, running between the stones, laying their hands on each of them. One by one, members of the crew, their faces alive with amazement and disbelief, joined them – even Steve threw aside the Banshee and charged in to take part. One after another, ghosts erupted from the stones and took flight, celebrating their freedom above the circle.

'Ha! *Ha!*' Uncle Larry laughed, whooping with delight, as if all his birthdays had come at once. 'This is amazing! Incredible!'

Angela stood watching in stunned disbelief. She seemed on the brink of a fit. The two cameramen glanced at each other, then started to set down their cameras, looking to run in and join in the fun.

Angela shot them a dagger-like glare. 'Don't you dare! Don't even think about it!' She gesticulated at the chaos. 'Do your job! I haven't the *faintest* idea what's happening but I do know I want it all on film!'

Adam and Lana laughed. As Uncle Larry and the rest of the crew raced from stone to stone, they made for the one they had touched on that first stormy night at the circle.

Together, at exactly the same moment, they laid their hands on the surface and waited to hear their friend's familiar chuckle.

15

Once again, the small army of ghosts whipped around the stones in a phantasmal frenzy, while Uncle Larry pointed and stared in wonder, leaping about almost as excitedly as the spectres themselves. It was like the ghostly equivalent of a fireworks display.

'They are *real*! These are real ghosts, ladies and gentlemen, and we have set them free here tonight! May all these wonderful spirits find peace! And may every one of you at home remember this sight for a long, long time!'

And as the camera lingered on the aerial display, the credits rolled and that was the end of another episode of *Fright Night*.

'So,' said Uncle Larry, sitting forward in his armchair and slapping his knees, 'what did you think?' He hauled himself up and walked over to switch off the TV. It was an antiquated box from before the days of remote control, with a wood-effect casing and an indoor aerial that always looked bent out of shape – whatever its original shape had been. Several times during the show, Uncle Larry had been forced to restore the reception with a good thump.

'Fantastic!' said Lana, her face lit up by a bright-eyed smile.

'Best episode ever!' said Adam.

'I admit, I wanted to dub over the final shots with a concluding line, something about now that these spirits had been set free, would the Shrieking Stones of Bray ever shriek again?' Uncle Larry sighed ruefully, returning to his chair. 'But Angela thought it better to stick with all that stuff I was babbling in the heat of the moment.'

'You let her have her way?' asked Lana, with a hint of a tease.

Uncle Larry missed the point as usual. 'Well, *why not*, I thought. She was in a good mood – once she'd got over the initial shock. She was happy.'

'Wow. Ghosts are one thing, but Angela being happy . . .' Adam winked at his sister. 'That really is unbelievable!'

'Indeed,' said Uncle Larry. 'She thinks this will do rather well in the ratings. Beat off the *Ghosts Unlimited* competition for one week, anyway.'

'They'll seem pretty limited next to that lot,' Lana assured her uncle.

Adam laughed. 'And she still didn't believe it, did she?'

Adam was remembering Angela's face as her gaze tried to follow the ghosts looping around each other above the stones. 'She thought it was some effect Steve had rigged up instead of the Banshee.'

'Yes, she thought he'd done it with lasers or something,' giggled Lana. 'Wanted to see a – what was it, Uncle Larry?'

'Cost analysis!' Uncle Larry joined in the laughter. 'She wanted to know what it cost us! It was priceless, that's what I should have said. And I told Steve to go ahead and take the credit as far as Angela was concerned. Poor man suffers enough working for her.'

'So, where to next?' Lana asked curiously.

'Hmm. Good question. I'm expecting a call from Angela tomorrow with next week's destination. The world is our oyster,' said Uncle Larry. Then he frowned. 'Although I'm not sure the *Fright Night* budget will stretch to oysters. Anyway, who's for a cup of cocoa?'

'Ooh, yes please.'

'Me too!' Adam gave a thumbs up.

'Right then. Talk among yourselves. I'll see what I can rustle up!'

Uncle Larry sauntered off to the kitchen. There was an unusually easy confidence to his stride and it was good to see.

When he was out of sight, another figure faded steadily into view on the sofa, between Adam and Lana. He was quite faint, and the pattern of the cushions was clearly visible through him.

'I'm thirsty too,' said Fergus. 'Ask your uncle if he's got any spirits!'

'Oh, ha ha,' replied Adam. 'Your jokes get worse. So,' he added, gesturing at the now-empty television screen, 'what did you think of the programme?'

'Well, the ghosts put on a good show.' He cracked one of his familiar grins. 'But if you think those were impressive, you should see what else is out there . . .'

'Really?' said Adam, his eyes lighting up at the prospect.

'Oh yes,' Fergus tapped the side of his nose. 'You'll see.'

'And will you be coming with us?' asked Lana.

'Hmm, now that I really couldn't say.' He let his ghostly hands glide over the cushions either side of him. 'I might just hang around here. Your uncle might appreciate having a ghost around the place. Is there a bakery in this town?'

'There is,' said Lana, grinning.

Fergus had already gone back to studying the blank screen. He tipped his head this way and that, as though judging the television from a variety of angles. 'Anyway, never mind ghosts and all, this "telly-vision" thing of yours is a miracle and a half, if you ask me. I could get used to all this modern luxury.'

Adam and Lana looked at each other, both wondering whether to tell Fergus about remote controls and wall-mounted high-definition TV screens. Or any of the other 'modern luxuries' that Uncle Larry had yet to take on.

Without a word, they both decided their new friend could learn about those things all in good time. They were each hoping he might be around for a while.

'TV's great,' admitted Lana.

'But if you think it's great to watch,' added Adam, 'it's going to be a whole lot more fun making it . . .'